Will   Irma   Taranee   Cornelia   Hay Lin

The Power of Five

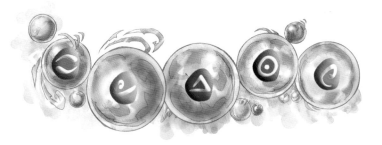

Adapted by ELIZABETH LENHARD

an imprint of
HYPERION BOOKS FOR CHILDREN
NEW YORK

W.I.T.C.H. Will Irma Taranee Cornelia Hay Lin is a trademark of Disney Enterprises, Inc.
Volo® is a registered trademark of Disney Enterprises, Inc.
Volo/Hyperion Books for Children are imprints of Disney Children's Group, L.L.C.

Printed in the United States of America

5 7 9 10 8 6 4

This book is set in 12/16.5 Hiroshige Book.
ISBN 0-7868-5257-7
Visit www.clubwitch.com

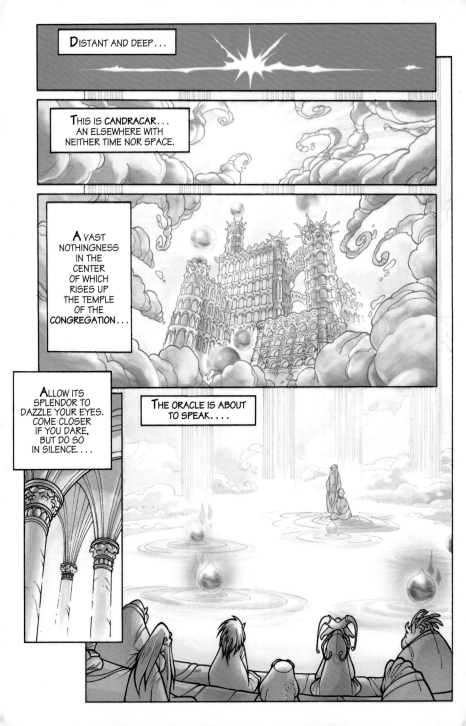

DISTANT AND DEEP...

THIS IS CANDRACAR...
AN ELSEWHERE WITH
NEITHER TIME NOR SPACE.

A VAST
NOTHINGNESS
IN THE
CENTER
OF WHICH
RISES UP
THE TEMPLE
OF THE
CONGREGATION...

ALLOW ITS
SPLENDOR TO
DAZZLE YOUR EYES.
COME CLOSER
IF YOU DARE,
BUT DO SO
IN SILENCE. . . .

THE ORACLE IS ABOUT
TO SPEAK. . . .

AAAGH!

WAKE UP, WILL! DID YOU HAVE A BAD DREAM, HONEY?

HOW SCARY! THERE WAS... THERE WAS A TERRIBLE STORM.

LOOKS LIKE IT'S RAINING CATS AND DOGS JUST ABOUT EVERYWHERE!

...WAVES OF TERRIBLE WEATHER CONTINUE TO HIT THE ENTIRE COUNTRY ON THE COAST...

CLICK

AND THIS WOULD BE HEATHERFIELD?

WELL, I'LL ADMIT, SEEN LIKE THIS, IT DOESN'T MAKE A GREAT IMPRESSION, BUT I'M SURE THAT TOMORROW IT'LL LOOK A LOT BETTER.

TOMORROW IS MY FIRST DAY OF SCHOOL, MOM.

OKAY, SO LET'S SAY THE DAY AFTER TOMORROW!

"I KNEW SHE WOULD COME, VATHEK...."

"SHE DETESTS THIS CITY, BUT SHE'LL SURVIVE."

YES, I'M CERTAIN THAT THIS GIRL AND I SHALL GET ALONG WELL, OLD FRIEND!

IT WILL BE A PLEASURE TO DESTROY HER!

ONE

Taranee Cook walked into the courtyard of her new school. She cringed as she looked at the sign looming over the entrance—a big, green archway that read SHEFFIELD INSTITUTE.

Institute. Taranee still wasn't used to that word. She remembered when her parents had told her the name of her new school.

Oh, yeah, Taranee thought, rolling her eyes behind her tiny, round specs. That was just before they made me pack up my entire life and move to a new city where the air always smells like salt water and the sidewalks are overflowing with skinny fashion models.

"The Sheffield Institute's one of the best private schools in Heatherfield," her mother had said, nodding briskly.

"You're putting me in an institution?" Taranee had wailed back.

Turned out, a lot of schools in Heatherfield were called institutes. It was just one more way this city was totally different from Sesamo, Taranee's *real* hometown.

She shivered as she wended her way toward Sheffield's front door, tiptoeing around the puddles still left over from that thunderstorm the night before. It had been a wicked downpour. Taranee must have spent an hour watching the lightning bolts zapping the ocean just beyond her bedroom window. With every strike, the lightning had seemed to inch a bit closer to her new cliffside house. But for some reason, Taranee had barely flinched.

Scared of fire? she thought. Not even. Scared is knowing that the tofu stir-fry Mom packed for me is going to be reeking by noon. Which means the stylish Sheffieldians will have yet another reason not to sit with me at lunch. The first reason being, of course, that they don't know I'm alive.

Taranee hopped around another puddle. But for all the leftover rainwater this morning, one would never know the storm had happened. The sun was shining and the sky was so blue it didn't look real. The stream of kids trotting up the school's stone steps all seemed to be wearing the latest fashions.

Just looking at all those strangers laughing and shouting hello to each other as they rushed into the school made Taranee shiver again. It was only her third day of school, and she was already dreading it. She yanked the cuffs of her orange turtleneck over her hands and gazed up at the Euro-style pink stucco building, complete with a mottled green copper roof and a big clock. A big clock that read 8:08. As in, two minutes till she'd be late for history class.

By the time she made it into Sheffield's main hallway, most of the kids had rushed off to class. Taranee caught her breath and made a dash for the big marble staircase. She was just about to launch herself onto the bottom step when she skidded to a confused stop.

"Oh, man . . ." she whispered. "I have no idea where to go!"

After only two days at Sheffield, Taranee realized, as dread swirled in her stomach, that she still hadn't mastered the maze that was her class schedule.

She tore open her kente-cloth book bag and began pawing through it. Tofu in Tupperware. Lip gloss. Eyeglass cleaner. Two shiny, new notebooks. And her schedule? Nowhere to be found.

Just when Taranee was breaking into a cold sweat, she heard the familiar *clomp-squeak-clomp-squeak* of frantically late sneakers behind her. She glanced up to see yet another stranger. But this one was a skinny girl with half a dozen cowlicks in her red hair and a chest that was almost as flat at Taranee's. She looked lost, too. The girl dug her schedule out of her jeans pocket and blinked at it. Then she spun around looking for an arrow, a trap door, a sign from the heavens—anything to save her from the dreaded first day of school. (How did Taranee know this? That had been *her*, forty-eight hours ago. She recognized the signs.)

Finally, the new kid's brown eyes flashed. She threw out her hands and screeched, "So, what does a girl have to do to get to room 304?"

Taranee grinned as the girl stomped her green sneakered foot in frustration.

"How to get to room 304?" she answered. "Hope to get promoted out of room 303, maybe."

The girl's skinny shoulders shot up to her ears as she spun around to stare at Taranee. Taranee tried to act casual. She didn't want the new kid to think she was *too* excited to be making actual human contact or anything.

"Two days ago, I had the same look on my face," Taranee said, tossing the longest of her randomly assorted, beaded braids over her shoulder. "I'm new, too. My name's Taranee."

"Nice to meet you," the girl said quietly. Slowly, her shoulders unclenched themselves. "I'm Will."

Taranee felt herself thrill inside. New-friend moment, she thought. Totally worth being late to class.

"Would you *please* explain what you're still doing out here in the hallway, young ladies?!"

Taranee cringed, and Will's shoulders shot back up to her ears.

"It's the principal," Taranee whispered to the terrified newbie, as the source of that very angry voice bustled toward them. "Mrs. Knickerbocker."

Ugh! Being late to history class, Taranee thought. That's no biggie. But a discipline session with Sheffield's big cheese? Taranee tried to think of things she'd rather do. Drink warm milk? Run a three-minute mile?

Ugh. Taranee shuddered. Okay, even doing time with Mrs. Knickerbocker is better than that, she thought.

Mrs. Knickerbocker stalked around the school with her ample chest thrust out before her and her even more ample backside swishing from side to side with terrifying force. It reminded Taranee of the swirling brushes of a street sweeper, dead set on ridding the hallways of filth (otherwise known as loitering students).

And then there was Mrs. Knickerbocker's hair. It was fascinating—a towering, shellacked pompadour. Snowy white. As translucent as spiderwebs. It was definitely one of the wildest old-people oddities Taranee had ever seen. She couldn't help staring at the stiffly glistening beehive as Mrs. Knickerbocker pointed a plump finger toward the east hallway.

Oh, yeah, Taranee suddenly remembered. *That's* where my history class is. . . .

"Lessons have already begun, Miss Cook," Mrs. Knickerbocker sputtered. "Straight to class."

Taranee was one step ahead of her. She'd already spun around and begun hurrying away.

She glanced over her shoulder as she slunk down the hallway.

Poor newbie, she thought, watching Will grin nervously up at the principal. I wonder what lunch period she has.

"As for you . . ." Mrs. Knickerbocker was saying, leering down at Will.

"M-m-my name is Will Vandom, ma'am," Will said, flashing the woman with the widest, fakest cheesy grin Taranee had ever seen. She liked Will already. "I think I'm a bit lost."

"Miss Vandom," the principal announced. "We're off to a bad start!"

Taranee sighed as she saw Will's chin drop to her chest. She knew *exactly* how the new kid must have felt: gawkily, nauseatingly, please-let-the-floor-open-up-and-swallow-me bad.

Come to think of it, Taranee thought as she finally located her history class and walked inside, that's just about how I feel right about now.

Taranee gave an embarrassed little wave at the twenty-one pairs of eyeballs that were, well, eyeballing her as she stumbled through the door. She looked wildly around the room, searching for an empty desk. Luckily, there was one right behind two girls she already recognized.

She had two other classes with them. They usually sat in the back of the room, the better to keep up their constant, whispered gossip sessions. Taranee was a little suspicious of the sassy early bloomer with the tousled, brown hair and pug nose, but she liked the Asian kid with the kooky clothes. Today—the kid was using a pair of green, bubbly goggles as a headband. The goggles clashed with her fuchsia sweatshirt in the most brazen way. She was beyond cool.

"Better late than never, Miss Cook," Mr. Collins called out from the blackboard. Even from the back of the room, Taranee could see his thick, red mustache twitching with amusement.

"Students are always welcome here," he continued. "Especially on days when there's a pop quiz!"

"A pop quiz?" the early bloomer cried. "Yesterday you said there would be a review!"

"I lied," Mr. Collins said, skulking down the aisle with another mustache-shimmying smile. He leered with vampirelike glee at the girl and said, "You should know by now, Irma, that we history teachers are mean by nature."

The Asian girl giggled and gave the early bloomer—Irma—a wink.

"I thought that was only math teachers," she piped up cheerfully.

Irma, meanwhile, was pouting big time. She slumped onto her desk and whispered, "This is just plain *cruel*. It's completely different."

Taranee sank into her desk chair and searched for her history book in her book bag. Actually, she felt grateful. In one fell swoop, Irma had shifted all the attention away from Taranee and onto herself.

Perhaps more attention than she'd bargained for.

"Why so upset?" Goggle Girl whispered to Irma. "Doesn't your spell work anymore?"

Taranee blinked. Spell?

Irma blinked, too. Then she glared at her friend.

"What on earth are you talking about?" she muttered, narrowing her blue eyes to malevolent slits.

"Oh, come on," Goggle Girl said, giving Irma's shoulder a playful nudge. "I mean rigging the quizzes."

"Did you say 'rigging the quizzes'?" Taranee whispered over Irma's shoulder. As soon as the question left her mouth, she gritted her teeth.

Way to go, she thought. As if I don't have enough black marks with Knickerbocker today. Now I have to walk into the middle of a cheating scandal.

Of course, Irma's reaction was no surprise. She whirled around and clamped her hand over her friend's grin.

"She didn't say anything," Irma said, somehow managing to glare at Taranee and Goggle Girl in one sweeping motion. "She just likes the sound of her own voice."

"Rmmmph," Goggle Girl gasped, before she squirmed her face out of Irma's palm. A second later, Irma unleashed a piercing yowl. She snatched her hand away from Goggle Girl and started shaking it around. She wiped it on her sweater with exaggerated disgust. Then she waved it high in the air.

"What's going on back there?" Mr. Collins yelled.

"Mr. Collins!" Irma yelled back. "Hay Lin bit me!"

Taranee stifled a snort of laughter while Hay Lin fiddled with one of her long, glossy pigtails and fluttered her eyelashes innocently.

Clearly, Mr. Collins knew how to play dumb, too. Ignoring Irma's bite marks, he simply homed in on her hand.

"That's a raised hand," he said. "Congratulations, Irma. I needed a volunteer, and it looks like I've found one."

"Burn!" Taranee whispered to herself. She'd learned the antique dis from Peter, her surfer-dude brother. And never had it been more appropriate than at this moment.

As Mr. Collins began to ponder his quiz question, Irma's injured hand started trembling. She sank into her chair.

"B-b-but that's not fair," she squeaked.

Hay Lin just giggled again and turned to Taranee.

"Watch and learn," she whispered from behind her hand. She wore a glittery purple ring that sparkled in the fluorescent light. "When Irma's quizzed, first she gets angry. Then she gets desperate. Then she shuts her eyes tight, crosses her fingers . . ."

"Shut up!" Irma snapped.

That would be "angry," Taranee thought.

"I didn't study at all," Irma whined to Hay Lin. "All I know is a little about Charles the Great."

Hel-lo, desperation, Taranee thought. Then Irma did just as Hay Lin had predicted. She laced her fingers together, clenched her eyes shut, and began chanting.

"Ask me about Charles the Great," she breathed in a rush. "Please-oh-please-oh-please-oh . . ."

Hay Lin continued to narrate to Taranee.

"See? And if there's only one single thing she's studied, that's exactly what the teacher is going to ask her about," she said. "I don't know how she does it. All I know for sure is that it works every time."

Taranee was . . . totally confused. So, it wasn't cheating that Hay Lin was talking about. She was saying Irma had . . . what? Some psychic power? A voodoo spell? A chunk of kryptonite hanging from her neck?

All three girls stared hard at Mr. Collins as he scanned his textbook.

"Hmmm," he said.

Charles the Great? Taranee thought.

"Let's see here," Mr. Collins muttered with agonizing casualness.

"Charles the Great," Hay Lin whispered impishly.

"Irma Lair . . ." Mr. Collins began.

"Charles the Great," Irma pleaded in a hoarse whisper.

"Why don't you tell us," Mr. Collins demanded finally, "about Charles the Great?"

"Yes!" Hay Lin cried, bursting into loud laughter. It would have been a sure detention-getter if Mr. Collins hadn't been so focused on Irma.

Irma, meanwhile, practically clapped her hands with glee as she launched into a long, show-offy speech about some Holy Roman emperor.

Not that Taranee listened to a word. She was too busy freaking. Maybe she had much more to fear from this curvy in-crowder than school yard snubbing.

Maybe . . . Taranee thought. But before she let the idea form fully in her mind, she shook her head hard enough to make her braids click together.

What was she thinking? That Irma, with her hippie, flower-power jewelry was . . . magical?

"Naw," Taranee muttered, slumping back in her desk chair with yet another shiver. "That's just not possible."

TWO

When Sheffield's final bell rang, Cornelia Hale looked down at her notebook page.

It was blank.

There was a physics test in three days, and Cornelia hadn't taken one note. In fact, she'd heard not one word of Mr. Temple's lecture.

Where have I been for the last fifty minutes? Cornelia wondered, blinking sleepily as she began to put her notebook and pens into her magenta messenger's bag. A long lock of blond hair fell over her eyes, and she shook it away impatiently.

I wish my hair wasn't so straight, she thought irritably, shoving the lock behind her ear even though she knew it would slither back into her face in about three seconds.

And then Cornelia felt a chill. Because suddenly she realized where the past hour had gone.

She'd been doing it again.

It had begun so gradually, Cornelia couldn't even remember when it had started. In fact, she didn't really know what *it* was. Not exactly. But she remembered the first time she'd been aware of it.

She'd been in English class. Martin Tubbs had been droning on about the symbolism of the night in *Huckleberry Finn*. Cornelia had sighed heavily—leave it to four-eyed Martin to find something obscure, then analyze it to death.

I wish it was night now, Cornelia had thought wearily. Then this whole, lame school thing would just be a distant mem—

Huh?

Just over her head, Cornelia had heard a sputter, then a pop. And then the classroom had gone dark.

Their teacher, Mrs. Nelson, leapt out of her chair.

"There must be a blown fuse," she'd said, going to the classroom door and looking out the window. "Although . . . that's funny. Ours seems to be the only classroom without light. Sit quietly, and I'll go get the janitor."

Of course, the class practically threw a party when Mrs. Nelson left. There was *nothing* like a reprieve in the last ten minutes of an excruciating English lecture. Cornelia had gotten up from her desk with a big grin and done a few stretches. (Being a figure skater, she craved constant motion.) Then she'd loped over to her friend Elyon's desk to show her the new lip gloss she'd bought the day before.

But, behind her happiness, Cornelia had felt a tiny kernel of unease. She'd glanced up at the dark, slightly hissing fluorescent lights. And a tremulous, almost silent voice in the back of her head had whispered, "Did I do that?"

That's when she'd suddenly remembered the broken pencil that had seemed to have sharpened itself, the bell that had rung just a few minutes early, the boy who had smiled at her *just* when she had willed him to.

And just now, during her physics lecture, Cornelia realized with a start, something even stranger had happened. She'd been staring out the window, gazing at the green-red leaves of a maple tree as they fluttered in the breeze. But then the leaves had begun to swirl around and form shapes. First she'd seen a squirrel. Then the face of a cute guy, winking at her. And then her little sister, Lilian, sneering. But when Cornelia had wished to see the cute boy again, there he'd been.

Part of Cornelia knew that, somehow, she was making these things happen. But most of her, the *real* her, the one who got things *done* instead of daydreaming her days away, managed to shake the knowledge from her head every time it wormed its way in.

It's not true, she told herself. Not true, not true, not true—impossible. She'd listened to enough physics lectures to know *that*.

Cornelia knew what would clear these thoughts from her head immediately—people. She headed out of the classroom to join the throng of kids in the hall. Most of them were already slamming their locker doors shut and running, not walking, toward every available exit door.

Cornelia noticed several people—most of them boys—glancing her way as they passed by. She shrugged it off. She knew she was part of

Sheffield's Infielders. As opposed to the Outfielders, as the school's rebels and misfits were known. Or the dreaded snufilupigi—invisible to all.

So, she was popular—big whoop. Cornelia didn't put too much stock in it. She knew who her *real* friends were. Friends like Elyon, whom she'd just spotted down the hall. She was plodding slowly through the crowd, looking even more wistful than usual.

Just as Cornelia started to wave to her, she was swept up into the whirlwind of Hay Lin and Irma.

"Ha!" Hay Lin was saying to Irma as they scurried out of their history class. "I can't believe you did it again!"

"Hey! It's a secret," Irma said, glaring at Hay Lin, whose slouchy jacket was falling off her skinny shoulders as usual. "You can't go around telling the whole school."

Then why are you talking it about it so loudly? Cornelia wondered. Then she pasted on a smile and turned to her buds.

"What can't she tell us?" she asked Hay Lin.

"Cornelia!" Hay Lin squealed. "The remote-control quizzes. She did it again."

Cornelia hid a tiny smile by turning to open her locker.

Remote-control quizzes, she thought with a little laugh. Irma thinks she's a big shot. But she's just a beginner. If she only knew what I can do.

For an instant, her mind flashed upon the cute, brown-eyed boy with the flouncy hair who'd appeared in the swirling leaves outside her classroom window. She felt as if she'd seen him before. Perhaps in a dream . . .

Then Cornelia shook her head sharply.

Impossible, remember? she admonished herself. She scowled into the mirror hanging inside her locker door, narrowing her blue eyes to slits. Then she slammed her locker door shut and spun around in time to see Hay Lin waving at an African American girl in an orange turtleneck and a cockeyed assemblage of beaded braids.

"See you tomorrow," Hay Lin called to the girl.

"Who was that?" Cornelia asked, watching the girl cautiously negotiate the pack of Sheffielders barreling through the door.

"Her name's Taranee. One of the new arrivals," Hay Lin said. "The other one is in class with you and Elyon, right?"

"Yeah," Cornelia said, noticing that Elyon had finally made her way through the throng and reached them. "I think her name's Will. But ask Elyon. She always has all the news."

Not that you could tell this afternoon. Elyon's eyes were downcast and her straw-colored bangs were even more shagged out than usual.

"Hi, guys," she practically whimpered. Then she fell into step with them as they all trooped out of school. Irma put a finger beneath Elyon's chin and turned her face toward hers, staring deep into Elyon's pale blue eyes.

"Look at me," Irma said. Then she nodded and glanced at Cornelia and Hay Lin.

"I've already seen this face before," she said.

"Me, too," Cornelia joked. "It was in a doc-umentary about Easter Island." She stuck out her lower lip and glowered.

"Oh, no, Cornelia," Irma said, contradicting her as usual. She ducked behind Elyon and pointed at her wan expression with mock concern. "I recognize a *flunked* look when I see one. And I'd say that what we have here is a big, fat, hairy *F*!"

Elyon yanked herself out of Irma's clutches and glared at her.

"All right, already," she said through gritted teeth. "I got a bad grade in math. Satisfied?"

"Of course, I am!" Irma said. "Because you know what that means, right?"

Uh-oh, Cornelia thought with a grin. Here it comes.

"Punishment!" Irma and Hay Lin screamed. They grabbed Elyon by the elbows and began to drag her through the Sheffield arch. Elyon made the most of her suffering, sighing heavily, rolling her eyes, dragging her feet—the whole bit.

"Come on," she complained. "You could look the other way, just this once."

"The law's the law, Elyon," Cornelia said with a giggle. "You know the rules of the group."

"And for a really terrible grade, we need something really nasty!" Irma said.

Suddenly, Cornelia had a stroke of genius. She gave Elyon a sidelong glance and then put on a puzzled look.

"Hmm, that's strange, though," she said. "I thought Matt-ematics was your favorite subject!"

Elyon stopped in her tracks and gasped.

"Leave Matt out of this," she cried.

"Of course!" Hay Lin said, bouncing tauntingly in front of Elyon. "He'll be your punishment. You'll have to convince the biggest hottie in the school to study with you."

"Begging and pleading," Irma added.

Cornelia covered her mouth to keep from guffawing. After all, she was probably the only one here who knew how big a crush Elyon had on Matt Olsen, who was scruffy and painfully cute, even if he was married to his guitar.

Hay Lin put her fists on her bony hips and swung around to face Irma.

"Let's get this straight, Irma," she said. "Either Elyon begs or she pleads."

"She should beg," Irma decided, nodding forcefully. "I said it first."

"And if we had her beg pleadingly?" Hay Lin proposed.

"That's silly!"

"But it's a compromise!"

Who needs *Mad TV* when you've got these goofy friends, Cornelia thought, letting one chuckle escape her pink-glossed lips before she gave Elyon a wave.

"Good luck," she called as Elyon slumped over in defeat. Then she turned left and followed the Institute's wrought-iron fence down the sidewalk. She'd parked her bike at the rack around the corner.

As she strolled along, feeling the breeze ripple her long lime-green skirt, she gave a little sigh. The change in season always made Cornelia a little sad, especially when summer gave way to fall. Cornelia couldn't help taking it a little personally when the trees lost their leaves. She knew it was silly, but she felt for those trees in the winter, all bare-limbed and damp and chilly. They seemed so . . . vulnerable. Leaves were like insulation, like the cozy, blue turtleneck she'd put on for her bike ride home.

A girl's yell jolted Cornelia out of her daydream.

Okay, time to ditch the vulnerable thoughts, she said to herself. Something's going down by the bike rack.

Another girl's voice, shrill as a bird, joined the first. Cornelia sped up.

What's going *on* over there? she wondered angrily.

As she rounded the corner, she saw one of the girls—hey, it was Taranee, the new kid in the orange sweater. Crouching on the sidewalk next to Taranee was the other new girl—Will. And they were both glaring at . . . ugh, Uriah's gang of thugs. Greasy hair, lots of zits, tattered skate duds, and a collective I.Q. of about 22.

They'd be the terror of Sheffield if they weren't so uncreative, Cornelia thought with a sigh. As it is, they're just a major pain in the neck.

This time, the thugs had tangled a bunch of bikes into an elaborate knot. Cornelia had seen it all before. But she wasn't sure if Taranee could handle it. She'd seemed pretty timid in the hallway.

"Did you guys do this?" Taranee demanded while Will yanked at one of the bikes angrily.

Oh, Cornelia thought, I guess she *can* hold her own.

"Hee-hee!" Kurt squealed. He was the tubby one with scuzzy brown hair. He and Laurent, with his blond buzz cut and barrel chest, were two dumb, giggling peas in a pod.

"Looks like somebody's going to be walking home today!" he teased.

Cornelia couldn't help noticing that Nigel, the only halfway presentable member of Uriah's crew, stood by silently. He issued no taunts, no name-calling. In fact, he looked a bit bewildered.

Kurt, on the other hand, was laughing so hard he was snorting like a pig. His fuzzy brown eyebrows waggled tauntingly at the new girls.

"So, you think that's funny, do you?" Will growled.

"Could be," Kurt bellowed. Then his eyebrows started wiggling . . . in a different way. He leered at Will.

"You're new here, aren't you?" Uriah said. "You're cute!"

"And you're the same old lamebrain, Uriah!" Cornelia burst out as she stepped over to the gang and tapped their leader on his bony shoulder. He spun around and stared at her, giving her way too close a view of his oily chin, his overgelled red spikes, and his pimply nose. Cornelia threw her shoulders back and returned his stare. She pointed at Uriah and then pointed at her blue bike, which was twisted around Will's red one.

"Is that my bike in the middle of that mess, too, Champ?" she asked him threateningly.

He scrunched his face into a snarl and blurted, "So deal with it! Let's move, guys."

Cowards, Cornelia thought, as the gang scurried after Uriah, guffawing and elbowing one another in the ribs before they disappeared around the corner.

"You've just met Uriah and his pals," Cornelia said to Will and Taranee. Ruefully, she blew a strand of hair out of her face.

"I sure could have done without it," Will said, biting her lip as she finally freed her bike tire from Taranee's handlebars.

"Don't worry," Cornelia replied breezily, pulling her own bike out of the mess. "Not everyone around here is like that. You'll see, at tonight's party."

Just saying that was enough to make Cornelia forget about all the creepiness and aggravation of the last hour. The Halloween dance. It was going to be sweet! She couldn't wait.

The new girls clearly did not agree.

"Oh, no! The party," Taranee cried.

"I forgot all about it," Will said. Then she turned and began working furiously on reattaching her bike seat to her bike, as if she'd like to *re*-forget all about it. Cornelia gazed at Will curiously. She had no idea what it was like to be the new kid in school. After all, she'd lived in Heatherfield all her life.

It must be awful, it occurred to her, not knowing anybody, not knowing how to get to places.

But Cornelia also thought it might be kind of awful to say something like that out loud. So, instead, she put on a cheerful smile and turned to the other new kid.

"Taranee, right?" she said, extending her hand. "I'm Cornelia."

"Nice to meet you," Taranee said with a shy smile.

"We're all meeting at the gym at eight o'clock," Cornelia told her. When she saw Taranee's smile begin to fade away, Cornelia squeezed her hand reassuringly.

"You'll see," she said. "It'll be a party you won't forget!"

"As far as I'm concerned," Will muttered behind Cornelia, "I just want to forget about today as soon as possible."

Cornelia decided to ignore the crack.

"And don't forget to wear a dress," she added. "Scary or wonderful or whatever. Just make sure it's special."

"I'll see what I can do," Taranee said drily, looking down at her slouchy jeans and baggy turtleneck.

Cornelia hopped onto her bike. Okay, so the new girls were a little frumpy. But that didn't matter—Cornelia had a hunch that underneath their new-kid crabbiness, they might be kind of cool.

She felt her usual "in control" mood returning as she propped a purple sneaker on her pedal.

"See you later, then," she said.

"I don't know, Cornelia," Will blurted suddenly, leaping to her feet with a panicked look in her huge, brown eyes. "I haven't been to a party in ages."

"Then this will be your chance to get back into the habit," Cornelia called over her shoulder as she began to ride away. Soon, she was halfway down the street, leaving behind the physics fiasco, Uriah, and all the other bummers of the school day. And suddenly, all she could feel was joy. She was surrounded by beautiful weather, her bike was picking up speed, and she had the coolest dress to wear to the dance tonight.

And, she realized, she might have two new friends on her hands. Turning around, she shot the girls a final grin and waved.

"Bye!" she called. And then she raced toward home.

THREE

Uriah stomped around the corner, pretending not to care if the guys were behind him or not. Besides, he knew they were. They always trailed him like loyal dogs. And besides—he could hear Kurt's fat feet clomping on the cement and Nigel's sneakers shuffling along timidly.

Nigel. What's *up* with that dude? Uriah thought, curling his thin upper lip. Nigel's been such a loser lately. Never wants to have any fun.

Thinking about losers, of course, sent Uriah straight back to his standoff with Cornelia Hale. He, uh, hadn't exactly won that battle.

But wait'll she sees what I've got in store for her, Uriah thought. And all the other Infielders who think they're better than me.

Uriah didn't know much, but he

knew there was one great equalizer in the world.

Fireworks.

And he had some.

Uriah snickered as his gang slumped into their usual after-school terrorizing positions on the front steps. Then they dug the day's junk-food supply out of their backpacks and commenced with some full-on slouching.

"Aaaaaarrrgggh," Laurent yawned loudly, five minutes later.

"Grrrgle," Kurt grunted through a mouthful of corn chips. "The show is over."

"Guys," Uriah cackled, jumping to his feet. "The show hasn't even started. Come with me."

As the last students trickled out of Sheffield, Uriah and his boys slithered back in. They sneaked—well, as much as one can sneak when the gang is made up of huge, sloppy lunks—into the west hallway and crept up to Uriah's locker.

Uriah nodded at his boys, and they each stationed themselves at a corner of the hallway. Uriah felt a surge of energy—he had power over these guys. Even if they were a bunch of duds, that meant something.

"The coast is clear, Uriah," Nigel said, looking over his shoulder.

"Keep on the lookout," Uriah snapped. Kurt glared down the hallway as Uriah quickly twirled through the combination on his locker. Then he reached in and paused. All three guys turned their attention to him.

"What is it?" Laurent whispered. At the moment of prime dramatic impact, Uriah pulled out three small rockets. He thrust them toward the boys and laughed maniacally.

"Whaddya say to these?" he said. "I took 'em, and a whole lot more, from my old man's boat."

"They're Bengal lights," Laurent said dully. "Flare rockets. Whaddya wanna do with them?"

Uriah sighed. He was working with amateurs here.

"At tonight's party," he explained slowly, "the school's taking care of the music and the eats."

"Yeah," Kurt said, totally bewildered.

"Yeah?" Nigel said edgily.

Uriah cackled again. Then he flashed his boys a triumphant grin.

"But," he announced, "I'll take care of the fireworks myself!"

FOUR

Irma sighed happily. She was in her favorite place in the whole world—the bathtub.

Well, actually her *favorite*, favorite place was the ocean. She grabbed every opportunity to hit Heatherfield Beach and soak up the salt water. She'd bodysurf for an hour or just float effortlessly on her back, feeling her hair fan out into the water, giggling when a fish skimmed by her toes.

So, let's call this her favorite place in her *house*, which, let's face it, was a pretty average, saltbox type of place. Certainly nothing like Cornelia's fancy high-rise apartment or Hay Lin's funky flat above her parents' Chinese restaurant.

Still, Irma's bathtub was glam.

She'd stacked every available surface with beautiful bottles of bubble bath and flowery salts and shells she'd collected from the beach. Sometimes she even propped her pet turtle, Leafy, on the tub's rim. He would dunk his claws into the hot bathwater and scowl at her over his little horny nose.

The two-hour soak was a key part of her getting-ready-for-a-big-night ritual. Sometimes, Irma wished it were the *only* part.

It wasn't that she was nervous about the party. That part would be a blast.

No, Irma told herself. It's the agonizing half-hour pawing through my closet that I'm dreading.

Irma dunked her head beneath the bathwater and blew a dramatic stream of bubbles. When she popped up, she swaddled her head in a pink towel and reached for the cordless.

"Hi!" Hay Lin's voice chirped through the phone.

"How'd you know it was me?" Irma asked.

"Didn't," Hay Lin said with a giggle. "I just wanted to psych out whoever it was. Whatsup?"

"I still don't know what to wear tonight," Irma wailed. "What about you?"

"No, I haven't decided yet what I'm going to wear," Hay Lin said. "But it's certainly going to be something spectacular."

Irma could just picture Hay Lin in her bedroom. She'd be perched in her favorite spot—the window seat—gazing out at the rain, totally oblivious to the chaos around her. And that chaos most likely consisted of, say, one Rollerblade and about a dozen comic books scattered on the floor, crusty paintbrushes drying next to her easel, and action figures hanging all over the computer terminal like little monkeys.

"All I can tell you," Hay Lin continued, "is that it's a new outfit and when I pass by, everyone's head will turn."

"Wow," Irma said, trailing her finger glumly through the bathwater. "Another creation by Grandma, huh? Is it gonna be ready on time?"

"Of course, it'll be ready by eight," Hay Lin said with a nervous laugh. "You'll see. It'll be something unique! Something extraordinary! Something . . . something *bewitching*. And with a couple of stitches, it'll be ready in ten minutes."

Then Irma heard a rustling and some quick, peppy footsteps.

"Right, Grandma?" she heard Hay Lin say.

"Ten minutes, as always."

That was Hay Lin's grandmother's voice—high-pitched, reedy, and thickly accented. The older woman both fascinated and frightened Irma. She was the tiniest grown-up Irma had ever seen, with the *biggest* ears she'd ever seen. They jutted out from her long, wispy white hair like a mother lion's—always cocked and listening.

Hay Lin was back to Irma.

"Well, I better hop in the bath myself," she said. "Just wait'll you see my dress!"

Click.

Irma tossed her cordless onto the fuzzy toilet seat and pulled her knees up beneath her chin. She turned on the hot-water tap to warm up the water a bit. Then she breathed deeply as steam swirled around her head. She let one hand drape across her knee, the fingertips just touching the water. As usual—lately—the connection sent a warm jolt flowing up her arm. It was almost like electricity. Not a shock, really. More like a pleasant power surge.

I'm really curious about her dress, Irma thought, as she wiggled her fingers lightly. Hay Lin is always full of ideas. As for me, as always,

I don't know what to wear! It should be something dark that fits the occasion. Something that matches my mood!

Irma stretched out her arm and dipped a single finger into the water. She twirled it around lightly.

I always get nervous when something that I don't understand happens, Irma thought unhappily.

Then, hesitantly, she raised her finger out of the water.

Yup—there it was. The water was rising out of the tub, like a cobra hypnotized by a snake charmer's music. Steadily, a thin stream of water bobbled through the air—coiling and flipping over itself. It was as if Irma were a conductor and her finger a baton.

Something really *incomprehensible* is going on here, she thought as the rocking rivulet danced past her eyes. She had more control over the water than she'd had at first. The day she'd discovered the water following her command—about two months earlier—Irma had, of course, lost her head. It was so exciting! Before she knew it, she'd created a small tidal wave, leaving the tub empty of everything but her shivering self and the bathwater sloshing all over the floor.

Since then, every bath had been a chance to experiment with this wild water dance. She'd gotten better and better. Now she could make fountains, whirlpools, and bubbles frolic obediently around her.

Should I talk to the others about this? Irma wondered as she flicked an overenthusiastic arc of water away from her hair.

"Maybe not," she muttered to herself. "After all, playing with water is so nice. It's so. . . so . . ."

Magical, she thought. Because she couldn't even bring herself to say the word out loud. It was too crazy. Of course, making six streams of water do the cancan out of the tub was just a little crazier than calling it magic, wasn't it?

Irma was just giggling to herself when a buzz kill barreled through the door in the form of her father's voice.

"IRMA!"

Splooosh! Splish! Splash!

Irma winced as her lovely cancan dancers collapsed into a big puddle on the floor. Her arching fountain missed its target and landed over by the sink. Her magical water was now just . . . wetness. All over the floor.

"Are you done?" her dad bellowed through the door from the hallway. "You've been in there for more than an hour!"

Irma sighed. I *had* to get a police sergeant for a dad, she thought. I couldn't have gotten, oh, a club DJ or a nice, laid-back hippie?

"Just a sec!" she called out. She jumped out of the tub and grabbed her fluffy pink towel, wrapping it around herself. Then she gaped at the monstrous puddles all over the floor.

"Come on," she whispered to the water. "Evaporate. You wouldn't want Dad to see this mess."

"Irma! I'm warning you! I'm losing my patience."

"H-here I am," Irma called back as sweetly as possible while she whipped the towel turban off her hair and began flapping it through the air, trying to clear the steam.

"IRMA!"

"I'm coming!"

She wrapped the towel back around her head, put on her best pout and indignantly slid open the bathroom door. Then she slipped her feet into her (okay, slightly damp) pink slippers and minced past her dad into the hallway.

"The next time, I'm going to break down the door," her father said to her back. But she didn't have to see his face to know he was teasing her. "You know I can do it!"

"Oh, yeah," Irma tossed over her shoulder. "And by what law, if you please? It's not a crime to take a two-hour bath."

Her dad grimaced and rolled his eyes. Then he squinted at her smooth hands. His bushy, steel-gray eyebrows got all smushy with confusion.

"If only you got pruny fingers like everyone else," he said, "you wouldn't act like this. But nooooo!"

Irma had to giggle. Her dad liked to growl a lot, but she knew he was just a big teddy bear. Annoying? Often. But Irma still had a soft spot for him. Sometimes, on their long walks down to the beach, she would even hold his hand. That is, if she was *sure* that no Infielders were lurking about to see.

"The little lady can stay in there soaking all afternoon like it was nothing," her dad went on. "Good grief."

"I know my rights, Inspector," Irma teased.

Then she saw her dad's eyes shift to the left—toward the bathroom!

Danger, she thought. Eye contact has been made. Proceed to bedroom—immediately!

"Irma . . ." her dad was growling as he poked his head into the bathroom for closer inspection. "There's a *lake* in here!"

"I'll only speak in the presence of my lawyer," Irma squeaked as she trotted down the hall. She slipped inside her bedroom door before her dad could get himself into lecture mode. Slamming the door behind her, she leaned against it and sighed.

"Whew," she muttered. "It's tough being a teenager."

Kicking her slippers off, Irma slouched over to her desk and sank into her chair. She rested her head on her forearms and gazed into the black, reptilian—yet somehow inviting—eyes of her pet turtle.

"I envy you, Leafy," she sighed. "I'd like to have a nice shell, just like yours. The same outfit, every day, for your entire life. But me? I have to choose!"

Leafy looked less than moved. He turned his back to her and swam over to a piece of lettuce he must have overlooked earlier.

Rolling her eyes, Irma flounced out of her chair and opened her armoire doors. Her favorite dress—the one with the ruffly collar, sheer flowy sleeves, and swirly skirt—suddenly looked just awful. It was yellow. Yellow! What *had* she been thinking?

"Why can't I ever find what I want," she complained, flopping backward to sprawl on her pink, smooshy comforter.

"A nice, dark blue dress!" she said. "Now, is that asking for too much? That's all I could wish for."

And then . . . something happened.

Irma felt a familiar thrum. Her fingertips and toes tingled, and she felt a little spark at the back of her neck. It was exactly the feeling that coursed through her when she was conducting her little water ballets. The strange thing was—there wasn't a speck of water in the room. Not unless you counted the murky puddle in the bottom of Leafy's bowl.

But suddenly, there was *something* in Irma's room. It looked like a firefly, and it was hovering right in front of her nose! Irma gasped and stared at it. Where had it come from?

As the little spark of light shimmered and danced before her bulging eyes, Irma realized it was decidedly blue.

Irma blinked and groped for an explanation. Was she seeing spots from gazing up at the lightbulb? Or maybe she was having a weird reaction to her lavender bubble bath.

Before Irma could come up with more theories, the sparkly, floaty thing flew away. It made a shimmering arc across the room, then swirled into the armoire.

And that's when her yellow dress, along with all the other clothes in her armoire—turned blue.

Navy blue. Just what Irma had asked for.

Stifling a scream, she leaped off the bed and slammed her armoire doors shut. She could feel her heart pounding through her fuzzy towel.

She had no idea what to make of this! She shook her head and tried to catch her breath, racking her brain for some logical explanation. But her mind remained stubbornly blank, except for one phrase, that irritating thing her mother always said to her when she was pouting: "Careful what you wish for!"

FIVE

Will watched Cornelia's long blond hair trail behind her as she rode off down the sunny street. She heaved a big sigh and then returned her attention to her bike seat.

Thwip.

Finally, it snapped into place.

Well, Will thought, I think that was the first thing to go right today. Of course, I never would have had to play bike surgeon in the first place if Uriah hadn't shown up. Jeez, I had to have a run-in with the school bully—*and* the principal—on my first day!

Will felt her shoulders sag wearily as she and Taranee walked their bikes around the corner. As they passed Sheffield's big courtyard, Will's eyes drifted over to the gym—a boxy, modern building next door to the school. The decorating committee was scurrying around like, well, kids on Halloween. One girl was trying to cram an enormous bunch of balloons through the double doors. A jock was teetering on the top of a ladder as he glued ominous black bats to the gym wall. And a whole throng of Sheffielders were slapping papier-mâché onto a giant jack-o'-lantern. Its jagged grin made Will shiver.

"I don't know if I feel like going to the party," Will said quietly as she straddled her bike. "I'm tired. And I might have to help my mom connect to the Internet."

The minute the words left her mouth, she cringed. Lame, lame, lame.

"Well," Taranee said, turning to eye Will, "if you're not going, I'm not going, either!"

Slowly, Will began pedaling down the sidewalk. Taranee rode along next to her.

Will knew she should fight to fit in at Heatherfield, the same way she fought to beat the clock at swimming practice or fought to get along with her mom, even when her mom was driving her crazy.

But the thing was, back in Fadden Hills,

where Will and her mom had lived until just yesterday, Will had gotten accustomed to *not* fighting. In fact, she'd sort of gone into hiding. Will and her mother both had.

The issue? Dad.

Dad refused to let go after the divorce. He called and called and called. He never gave Will's mom a moment's peace.

Finally, her mom had moved them to Heatherfield, where they had an unlisted phone number. And it had worked. There'd been no phone calls since they'd arrived. Not a one from Dad *or* Will's "friends" in Fadden Hills.

Will sighed a shuddery sigh. She couldn't even really accuse her friends of dissing her. After all, she'd been the first one to pull away. During her parents' messy divorce, Will had gotten more quiet, more timid. She definitely was not much fun to be around. She knew that was why her friends had stopped including her in their after-school burger runs and Friday night basketball games. And that was why not one of them had called to check in since she'd moved.

Will's mom said the silence was a relief. But when Will thought of all the quiet in their new apartment—a place right in the city that her mom had chosen for the twenty-four-hour security guard at the gate—she imagined being wrapped in a big down comforter. It was protecting her from the world, but at the same time, it was muffling her, too.

A Halloween party, Will thought. Well, that would be a way to come out from under the covers in full force, wouldn't it?

Before she could change her mind, she whipped her cell phone out of her sweatshirt pocket. Expertly, she dialed with one hand while she steered her bike with the other.

"Let's hear what the boss has to say," she said to Taranee as she mashed the SEND button with her thumb.

"Wow," Taranee said, her eyes widening behind her glasses. "You've got your own cell phone?"

"Yeah," Will said. "My mom works for Simultech. She's never at her desk. So . . . the cell phone is like my second mother."

Will glanced at the sky as the phone rang.

That's funny, she thought. Look at all those black clouds rolling in. Just a minute ago, the sun was blinding.

"Susan Vandom," her mother said, picking up after the third ring.

"Hi, it's m—"

"Will!" Her voice shifted from clipped and professional to warm and gooey in a millisecond. "How was the first day?!"

"Listen," Will said, wanting to avoid the whole first-day rehash for as long as possible. "There's going to be a party at school tonight, and—"

"Fabulous!" Her mother gushed. "That's a great place to make new friends, Will! What luck!"

"Wait," Will said, panic suddenly rising in her throat. She realized that she'd called her mom hoping to get some negative vibes. It would have been a perfect excuse to scrap the whole party plan.

But Will had forgotten how irritatingly cool her mother could be sometimes.

"I'll drive you!" she said.

"Would you let me—" Will stammered.

"You should wear that black halter dress."

"It's just that—"

"What?" Her mother interrupted again. "I assume it's a Halloween party? So the black will be perfect. Plus, Halloween is only your favorite holiday. Well, back when you were trick-or-treating it was, anyway."

"But—"

"I *knew* Heatherfield would be a great place for you," her mother said cheerfully. And suddenly Will knew—there was no getting out of this party. Not unless she wanted to totally worry her mom.

"Okay," Will said, feeling weary once again. "Talk to you later."

Will gave her cell phone a withering glare and pushed END. Then she stashed it back in her pocket and struggled to look at Taranee.

"Did she say no?" Taranee asked. Will could see a familiar seesaw between hope and fear in Taranee's eyes.

"She said yes," Will replied flatly.

"So . . . aren't you happy?"

Will cringed and shot Taranee a wobbly, totally fake grin.

"Can't you tell?" she said and crossed her eyes.

Taranee laughed out loud. And Will found herself smiling for real. For the first time, it occurred to her—maybe she wasn't totally alone in Heatherfield, after all. Maybe she and this fellow newbie could become fast friends.

Will grinned at her new bud. And Taranee responded with a squeal.

"Aaaigh," she cried, looking skyward. "It's raining!"

"Day complete," Will muttered as a fat raindrop hit her on the nose. Her one happy moment was being washed away by a sudden shower.

"I live on the next block," Taranee called as the rain quickly morphed from drizzle to downpour. "Want to come take shelter?"

"Sounds great to me!" Will said. She pedaled after Taranee. A minute later, they pulled up to Taranee's house, which was shiny, white, and ultramodern. It was all about crazy angles and glass bricks. The girls ran inside.

"Tea," Taranee declared, trotting to the kitchen and kicking her wet sneakers under the kidney-shaped, white island. "My parents are still at work, and my brother's probably at the beach. He's completely addicted to surfing. So, we've got the house to ourselves."

She filled a kettle with water and broke out a

couple of mugs and a can of instant chai tea. Then she flounced onto a tall stool and smiled at Will.

Will smiled back. And suddenly, they were deep into chat. They talked about Sesamo, where Taranee was from, and about Fadden Hills. They giggled as they recalled the bizarre bod of Mrs. Knickerbocker. And before Will knew it, an hour had gone by and the sun had reemerged.

"It's stopped raining!" Will said, peering through the kitchen's sliding glass doors in surprise. "I'd better be going. But thanks for having me over, Taranee."

Taranee slumped a little, gazing into the dregs of her chai.

"How are you going to look tonight?" she asked. "Scary or elegant?"

"I always look scary," Will said, pulling on her navy sweatshirt and swiping at her rain-damp red hair. "I've decided to try something new."

Taranee laughed as they headed outside. Will grabbed her bike off the front porch and bounced it down the steps.

"So," Will said, shrugging at Taranee, "I'll pick you up at seven-thirty, then."

Taranee shrugged back with a smile and

said, "On your bike?"

"By car. My mom will take us," Will said, knowing her mom would be psyched to meet her new bud.

"Great," Taranee said. "See you later, Will."

Will grinned and waved as she set off down the street. For a moment, she felt light as air, loving the sizzling sound her tires made as they skimmed over the wet sidewalk. But the minute Taranee faded from the little rearview mirror on her handlebars, Will felt her grin collapse. She frowned as wet leaves and twigs whipped around her pedaling feet. A mist still hung in the air, making her messy, chin-length locks even more lank than usual.

Maybe I spoke too soon, she wondered as she turned off Taranee's tree-lined street onto one of Heatherfield's main streets. I don't think an elegant dress was such a bright idea. I'd feel a lot better wearing a sweat suit.

She smiled wryly as she rode past a stretch of boutiques, the kind that sold exactly the sort of little, strapless nothings that Will could *not* picture herself wearing.

"I should ask around," she muttered. "Who knows if they sell evening sweats somewhere. If they exist, I bet they're sequined."

Just to make sure there *wasn't* such a thing as sparkled sweats, Will peered into the next window she passed. But she couldn't make out what was inside. All she saw was a reflection of her own whizzing bike wheels and—

"Huh?!" Will gasped. She grabbed her brakes and skidded to a halt. And then, she gaped into the window.

She blinked a few times.

Then she stared some more.

The reflection blinked and stared back at her. But that reflection wasn't her! Or was it?

The girl looking back at her was more like . . . a woman. Her hair was Will's same red mop, but it was straighter, chunkier, cooler. It seemed to flutter perfectly in a breeze that wasn't there. And the face—that was Will's, too, if you added cheekbones and plumped up the lips and put a cool knowingness in her eyes.

And then, there was that body. Her figure was definitely, um, *enhanced*. This fantasy Will was taller than the real Will and had curves at every spot where Will had angles and flat planes. Will's too long, baggy Adidas pants and red T-shirt had been replaced by a tight, belly-button-baring purple top with bell-shaped sleeves. And her long, muscular legs were wrapped in blue-and-turquoise-striped tights and amazingly rad, knee-high boots.

Her backpack, though she could still feel the straps looped around her shoulders, had disappeared from her reflection. And in its place were . . .

Wings.

They looked more flowery than feathery—thin, dark stalks dotted with delicate, translucent petals. As Will stared, the wings undulated lightly, swayed by the same invisible breeze as fantasy Will's mod hairdo.

Will's eyes traveled up and down, and up and down this bizarre reflection until she realized that she'd stopped breathing. She gasped, sucking in a gulp of air. Then, finally, she tore her eyes away from the window. She glanced around quickly to see if anyone else could see what she did, but luckily, this stretch of sidewalk was empty after the rain. She looked up at the sign above the window. No, it wasn't some freak show or occult shop. Just a shabby-looking place called Ye Olde Bookshop.

Almost against her will, Will's sneaker—or was it her purple leather boot?—found her bike pedal. She stood on the pedal so fast that the bike gave a little hop as it began speeding down the sidewalk.

Will pedaled as hard as she could. Her breath came in ragged gasps. She kept her eyes on the cement in front of her, not daring to even glance into any other window she passed. Already, her altered image was beginning to waver in her mind. Perhaps the day's stresses had warped her vision. Maybe fantasy Will hadn't been there at all!

The problem was, Will didn't feel as if she were hallucinating. Or even crazy. Slightly neurotic, yes. But unhinged? No.

Which meant that this figure, this alternate Will, had somehow been . . . real?

Will's mind was racing as fast as her bike. She shook her head, blinking her tousled hair out of her eyes. Through rattling teeth, she muttered, "Th-that can't be!"

SIX

Cornelia couldn't believe this was her life. She was standing in the upstairs hall of her apartment, actually wearing her dress for the party, and her mother was telling her she couldn't go out.

"Forget it, young lady," she was saying, glaring down at Cornelia through her oversized glasses. "Tonight, you're not going anywhere. At least, not until you've cleaned your room!"

The two of them glared through Cornelia's bedroom doorway. Okay, Cornelia had to admit it to herself, the room was a total sty. There were sweaters strewn on the floor and dangling off the dresser after that morning's what-should-I-wear-fest. Research for a biology report was scattered around her desk. Stuffed animals were crashed out at the foot of her unmade bed. Even her ice skates were tossed under the windowsill, and some of her old skating trophies were overturned.

Well, Cornelia thought, I like it that way. So sue me for being a free spirit.

Not that *that* approach would work with her rigid mother. Instead, Cornelia would opt for bargaining.

"Come on, Ma!" she yelled. "I'll do it tomorrow!"

"What's keeping you from doing it now?" her mother said, pursing her lips and crossing her arms. Through a haze of rage, Cornelia was dimly aware of how alike they must look. Both had heart-shaped faces with pointy chins thrust out in identical, angry pouts. Both had long, skinny arms crossed stubbornly over their chests.

This knowledge only made Cornelia angrier. "My genetic coding," she growled, "doesn't let me give in to blackmail!"

"As you like, Cornelia," her mother replied coolly. She turned her back on her daughter and began to head down the stairs to the open, high-ceilinged living room. "If this is a challenge, you're the one who's got everything to lose."

There's only one thing that could make this moment more completely annoying, Cornelia thought.

"Neat!" piped up a squeaky voice behind her.

And *that* would be her, she thought. She turned to glare at her sister, Lilian—six years old and irritating enough to be twins.

"Looks like tonight, we'll all be at home together, huh, big sister?" Lilian said. She sneered slyly up at Cornelia.

"Shut up, you little toad!" Cornelia yelled. Then she began to stomp toward her bedroom. Even stomping made her mad, because stomping on the Oriental rug made no noise whatsoever.

"Why can't rooms just clean themselves?" she groaned.

Slam!

Cornelia reared back in shock. Her bedroom door had just slammed in her face! She whipped around to see Lilian hopping down the stairs, making little toadlike noises.

"*Ribbit. Ribbit. Ribbit,*" Lilian said with each little hop.

Cornelia scowled. Lilian was just trying to get to her. And actually, it had worked. Because if Lilian was out here, that meant she hadn't slipped into Cornelia's room and locked her out. So, who had?

Cornelia frowned and reached for the brass doorknob. She rattled it back and forth, but the door wasn't budging.

Swiiiish, swooosh, swiiish.

Cornelia pressed her ear to her bedroom door. Something was definitely going on in there. It sounded like a wind flapping through crispy autumn leaves.

Feeling the first tremors of panic, Cornelia rattled the knob some more and banged the door with her shoulder.

"Urrrgh," she grunted. "Stupid door. I wonder why it won't . . . aaagh!"

Abruptly, the door opened and Cornelia almost fell inside her room.

Her . . . spotless room.

Cornelia clutched the doorknob weakly and gazed around. Her sweaters were folded on the foot of the bed, which was neatly made. The stuffed animals were smiling sweetly from her pillow. Her books were arranged in precise stacks on the desk. Her trophies had been polished and evenly spaced on the shelves. Her shoes were lined up like soldiers on the rug. Even the rug's fringes were neatly combed!

"Wow," Cornelia whispered. Whispering was all she could manage, considering that she was practically hyperventilating. She took baby steps into her gleaming room.

And that's when she felt a grin slowly work its way across her face.

I can't believe it, she thought, skimming a palm over her dust-free desk. All it took was the thought to make it happen! What Irma can do in class is nothing compared to what I've been able to do lately. In class, I control everything just by wanting it.

She walked, as if in a trance, to her newly organized vanity. Absently, she picked up her lip gloss and plopped a dab of it on her lower lip.

And now this, she thought, pursing her lips together contemplatively. Suddenly, she slumped onto the bed, creasing the perfect quilt.

What's happening to me? she wondered. What does this mean?

She glanced up and caught sight of herself in her vanity mirror. Her cheeks were as pink as her ethereal dress, and her eyes were sparkling. The sight of her dress made Cornelia remember what had started this whole mysterious room-cleaning. Her mother. Her *smug* mother, who thought Cornelia would be spending the night sulkily scrubbing her room.

Ha! Cornelia thought, bouncing off the bed. I know exactly what this means. It means I'm going to the Halloween party!

She went to the closet for her hot-pink shawl, which was—naturally—dangling from a hanger. She swept the shawl triumphantly around her shoulders and bounded out of her room. Then she hurried down to the living room and made a beeline for the front door.

"Cornelia!" her mother said.

Oops. Cornelia hadn't seen her mom lounging on the couch on the other side of their cavernous living room. Mom was reading a magazine, and Lilian was camped out next to her. "Where do you think you're going?"

"To the party," Cornelia called out breezily. "My room's clean."

As Cornelia bolted for the door, she saw her mother leap off the couch.

"Cornelia?" she called threateningly. "For your own sake, that had better be true. Cornelia!"

But Cornelia didn't stop. Why should she? It *was* true. Her room was clean.

Flying out the door, she practically crashed into her dad, who was just arriving home from work. He looked a little tired, but cheerful, in his damp raincoat and windswept brown hair.

"Hi, Pop!" Cornelia called, waving good-bye to him as she ran to catch the elevator.

"Hey," her father said jovially. "Did I miss something?"

There was no time to answer before the elevator doors closed, with Cornelia safely inside. She hit the lobby button and heaved a big sigh, leaning against the mirrored wall.

"Oh, boy, Pop," she muttered, shaking her head in disbelief. "Did you ever!"

SEVEN

After she'd arrived home from the most bizarre bike ride of her life, Will had gone to her room and collapsed onto her bed, banging into a half-unpacked box as she did. She kicked the box onto the floor and then looked around, gazing at this strange new room of hers. All she saw was chaos—rain-damp boxes, her frog collection scattered across her furniture, clothes tossed around the room.

The pile of clothes reminded her of what Cornelia had said before she rode away. "Don't forget to wear a dress.... Just make sure it's special."

A miniskirt, purple boots, and a pair of wings, Will thought. Well, *that's* pretty special.

Then Will shook her head. She just couldn't

forget the image she'd seen reflected in the bookshop window.

But she also couldn't *stand* to think about it. It was too much to handle today! Will flopped onto her stomach and stared at the phone on her nightstand. She loved her old-fashioned white phone—it was called the Princess style—and she loved her creaky, old, wooden night-stand. If she squinted at them hard, she could tune out everything else in this room. She could pretend that she was back home in Fadden Hills. And her phone was just about to ring. There'd be a bunch of friends giggling on the other end, inviting her out for a movie.

Ring, she willed the phone. Ring . . . ring . . .

Will awoke with a start and blinked blearily. The first thing she saw was her telephone—her utterly silent telephone.

It's *so* silent, Will thought, rolling over to the edge of the bed, that I must have dozed off for a minute. Rubbing one eye, she looked around for her frog with the clock in its belly. It was gone, just like the rest of her stuff—lost in the mess somewhere.

Yawning loudly, Will heaved herself off the

bed and stumbled to the window. Then she woke up completely.

It was pitch-black out! What *time* was it?!

She rushed into the hallway and glanced at the wall clock: 10:04! She'd fallen asleep for hours! With a yelp, Will ran into the bathroom, discarding clothes as she went. Then she jumped into the shower.

Five minutes later, she was rushing around her room in her underwear, her hair dripping into her eyes, looking desperately for something to wear.

After throwing the contents of about six boxes onto the floor, she unearthed a dress—a short, red velvet shift with wide shoulder straps. She pulled it over her head and spun in front of her full-length mirror.

Okay, this is not good, Will thought. She skimmed her hands over the dress, flattening it against her hips. She caught a hint of curve, but as soon as she let go, the dress hung away from her body again, as lifeless as ever.

She turned sideways. Okay, *that* was even more depressing. She was a two-by-four in red.

"Will!"

Her mom's voice startled her out of her

gloom. Will turned and glared at the door. She could just picture her mom leaning against it, rolling her big brown eyes and gazing down her long, Roman nose at her watch.

"It's super-late," her mom said through the door.

"Who cares about the party?" Will yelled, whipping the red dress off and clenching it in her fist. "I didn't want to go, anyway. You're the one who insisted."

She held the straps up to her shoulders, dangling the dress over her body. She glared down at the lifeless fabric.

"On top of that," she ranted, "I have *nothing* to wear. Everything makes me look like a surfboard and . . . and . . ."

Will's voice trailed off to a bewildered squeak as she caught a glimpse of her reflection in the mirror.

The face in the mirror wore Will's surprised expression. The hand clutched the withered, red velvet dress. But the body . . . once again, it was utterly foreign—tall and shapely, with a waist that nipped in and hips that flared out. Will's eyes traveled to her reflection's chest and blushed. This *had* to be a figment of her imagination.

"That's . . . that's not me," Will whispered, reaching out toward the mirror. The reflection's hand touched her own with strange, manicured fingers. Will stared at this . . . this ghost and was powerless to do anything but tremble.

"Will?"

In the top corner of the mirror, Will spotted her mother's face, peeking around her open door and gazing at her questioningly.

What will she think? Will thought in a nervous panic. *Her daughter has suddenly been replaced by a stranger!*

"Aaaaagh!" Will screamed, covering her face with the dress. "Don't come in! Don't come in!"

"What?!"

Will peeked out from behind her dress to see her mother, fully inside her room now. She was looking at Will in irritation. Will searched her mom's face for shock and horror, as well. But there was none.

Will bit her lower lip and glanced back at the mirror. She was back—the real Will, flat chest, knobby knees, and all. She looked disheveled, scared, and just a little bit nuts.

"Why aren't you dressed yet?" her mom

asked, glancing at her watch. She pointed at a filmy, black dress crumpled in the bottom of a box—Will's halter dress with the little rose at the neck. "Aren't you going to put that black one on? It used to be your favorite."

"The only thing in black that would look good on me is a garbage bag," Will said, feeling the sting of tears springing to her eyes.

"What are you talking about?" her mom said, gently laying a hand on Will's shoulder. "What's wrong?"

"I look like, no, I *am* a broomstick," Will said through a choked sob. She batted the red velvet dress angrily against her skinny leg.

But she had to admit, she felt a tiny bit better when her mother gave her shoulders a little squeeze.

"You are a special girl who will meet new special friends at the party, just as you are." Then she grabbed Will by the shoulders and turned her toward the mirror. Will looked at her mother. She saw a pretty woman with long, wavy black hair and big hoop earrings. And next to her, she saw a girl. A skinny girl with a scruffy head of hair and wan, red-rimmed eyes.

"Look at yourself, Will," her mother said. "You have to love yourself, because only in this way will you allow other people to appreciate your qualities."

Will squinted at her reflection. Was it *possible* to love herself in this state? She decided to give a small smile a try. She lifted a corner of her mouth.

Not bad.

She raised the other corner.

Will didn't want to admit it, but it *did* help.

She grabbed the black dress out of the box and held it up against her body. Not bad, again. *Definitely* better than that old red dress.

"Now, let's get going," her mom said. "The party won't last forever."

"And we have to pick up Taranee," Will added. Thankfully, Taranee was not mad about the late ride. She was happy that Will still wanted to go.

Twenty minutes later, Mrs. Vandom and the two girls pulled up at Sheffield. Will and Taranee hopped out of the car and waved good-bye to Will's mom, who hung her head out of the window and grinned.

"Have a great time," she called. "Hey,

Taranee, take good care of Will for me. She's a shy girl. Put a little fire into her!"

"See you later, Mom," Will said, feeling her cheeks go hot. She felt a surge of gratitude for Taranee's sweet smile. It would have been so easy to snort with laughter, point at Will and shriek, "Mama's girl!"

Instead, Taranee just waved at Mrs. Vandom and said, "Maybe I'm not the right person for the job, but I'll try!"

The girls followed the orange-and-black signs taped to fence posts, pillars, and any other available surface. They all pointed to the party. With each step closer to the pounding music and shrill chatter of the dance, Will's mouth got drier.

"We're still in time, Taranee," she hissed into her friend's ear. Or what would have been her ear if Taranee hadn't dressed as a sort of neopunk Amelia Earhart. She was wearing a leather aviator's cap, complete with goggles and earflaps, and a zebra-striped coat over her simple pink dress. "Let's turn around and get out of here."

"Looks like it's too late," Taranee said, sounding just as tremulous as Will did. "Cornelia!"

Will gasped and peeked over Taranee's shoulder. Yup—there was the blond goddess herself, looking as gorgeous as ever in a tiny purple camisole and voluminous pink skirt. She looked every bit the popular girl. But Cornelia's smile was as warm and welcoming as it had been that afternoon.

"Hours late," Cornelia said with a grin. "Fashionably late, you might say. That's okay. The party's just hitting its peak."

EIGHT

Irma looked down at the filmy, indigo skirt of her once-yellow dress and willed it to shimmy back and forth, or spin around or . . . *something*.

You're at a party, she told herself irritably. She glanced at the costumed kids milling around the gym in hockey masks and devil's horns and dramatic, flowing dresses. Cobalt Blue was on the stage, slamming out an Alicia Keys cover. The overhead lights had been covered with gold cellophane and candles burned in the rafters, giving the entire room a hazy yellow glow.

A party, Irma reminded herself again. As in *fun*? As in dancing and flirting with boys and raiding the cupcake platter?

But it's hard to dance when you're seething. Which is exactly what Irma had been doing ever since she made the mistake of confiding in her friends about her wardrobe's magical transformation. Hay Lin and Elyon had laughed so hard, they'd almost collapsed on the floor.

"Your dress turned from yellow to blue," Hay Lin snorted. She looked down at her own silky kimono, which was just as gorgeous as she'd promised. "And I'm actually a Japanese geisha."

"Next thing you know, she'll come to school as a blonde and tell us, 'I didn't dye it. It was *magic*,'" Elyon squealed.

Elyon's just picking on me to distract us from her punishment, Irma had thought angrily. She gave the band's lead singer, Matt Olsen—otherwise known as Elyon's big crush—an angry glare.

And now, to top it all off, Irma's friends weren't paying *any* attention to her. They'd all traipsed to the gym door to greet the new girls, Will and Taranee. Cornelia was planting a pointy black witch's hat onto Will's sheepish head.

"It's my fault we're late," Will said. "I lost track of time, and. . . ."

"Hear that, Irma?" Elyon said, turning to grin at her. She was dressed as an elf, or imp, or fairy—something mischievous, anyway. She wore a feathery green tunic and a crown of leaves. "This is what I call an original excuse!"

Hay Lin glanced at Irma and giggled.

"She got here late, too," she told Will and Taranee. "And do you want to know what excuse she made up?"

"There's nothing to laugh about," Irma retorted with a scowl. "All of the clothes in my wardrobe *did* change color."

Hay Lin and Elyon burst into another round of hysterical giggles. Irma squirmed some more. She knew if it had been anyone else telling such a crazy story, she'd be the one laughing loudest. But, well, the shoe was on the other foot now. And boy, did their laughing make Irma mad.

"It's the truth!" she yelled at Hay Lin and Elyon. "And if you don't want to believe it, that's your problem."

Will stepped in from the doorway and met Irma's eyes.

"I believe it," she said quietly.

Before Irma could flash her a grateful smile, Martin Tubbs appeared.

Martin! Any time Irma least wanted to see him, which was, well, pretty much always, there he was. And each time he was goofier than the last. Tonight he was wrapped in about a hundred yards of tattered bandages. Behind his Coke-bottle glasses, he blinked dreamily at Irma.

"Hi, Irma," he whispered. When she glared at him with what she hoped were icy eyes, he leaped back and whipped out a Polaroid camera. At least Martin *sometimes* knew how to read Irma's "get lost" signals.

"How about a picture, gals?" he called.

"Yeah!" Hay Lin cried. She slung her arms over Will's and Taranee's shoulders, and Elyon and Cornelia squeezed in. Then Hay Lin grabbed Irma and yanked her into the shot.

"I'll never tell you any secrets again," Irma hissed to Hay Lin. "So there!"

"Smile, ladies!" Hay Lin called, grinning into Martin's camera and pointedly ignoring Irma.

As soon as Martin's flashbulb popped, Cornelia and Taranee drifted off toward the refreshments, leaving Irma, Hay Lin, Will, and Elyon to groove to Cobalt Blue's throbbing music. The last note of Matt's song seemed to echo through the gym, causing Elyon to go all pale and trembly. Irma rolled her eyes and glanced at Will.

What's this? she thought. Looks like Will's getting a little misty-eyed, too!

Will gazed at Matt as he heaved his guitar out of the way and grabbed the microphone.

"Thirty minutes till midnight, my friends," he yelled into the mike. "Halloween is here! A big hello to the great pumpkin, yeah!"

"Oh . . ." Will said quietly.

Uh-oh, Irma thought. I smell a new crush!

"Cute, huh?" Hay Lin said to Will. "His name's Matt. He's the one that Elyon likes. He's a little older than us."

"I thought the older guys were all like Uriah," Will said breathily.

"Speaking of," Irma broke in, "hope you're not too hungry, Will. Uriah and his drones practically cleaned out the sandwich buffet earlier. Totally on Knickerbocker's radar, too. I heard her talking to them." Then Irma added in her best Mrs. Knickerbocker impersonation,

"'*Bon appétit*, boys. From the looks of your booty, I'd say you all like the buffet.' And then Uriah was all, 'It's not how it looks, Principal. We're only stocking up on our winter supplies.'"

"Ugh," Will said.

"That's what Knickerbocker thought," Irma continued happily. She *loved* when she had good gossip to dispense. "So she was all, 'I guess that means you're ready to spend another school year in hibernation? Excellent!'"

"Go, Knickerbocker," Hay Lin squealed with a laugh.

"Yeah, Uriah was really bugged," Irma giggled. "Haven't seen him since."

"But I *do* see someone new," Elyon interrupted. By now, their group had migrated further into the party. They were hanging in a cluster, halfway between the dance floor and the gym door. And walking through that door was a guy who looked so cool it was hard to believe he was in high school. He totally wasn't Irma's type, but even she couldn't help staring at him. He was so *dramatic*, with straight, silky brown hair that hung from a blue stocking cap all the way to his waist. He wore a long, deep purple coat and an angular turtleneck straight out of *Star Wars*. A bright pink mask hid his eyes, but Irma could still tell he was a hottie, with a chiseled chin; fine, small nose; and skin that was pale and perfect.

"So what do you think of that guy who just came in?" Elyon said. Irma could practically see Matt being erased from her mental crush book, to be quickly replaced by this mystery man.

"Never seen him before!" Hay Lin gasped. "He looks out of this world!"

"But he's wearing a mask," Cornelia said. She'd just returned from the snack table, empty-handed.

"He still looks out of this world," Hay Lin gushed.

"They all seem out of this world to you, Hay Lin," Irma said, giving her friend a sidelong glance.

"That's not true," Hay Lin retorted. "For example, the one who's walking up to you now is *uuuugly*."

"How about another picture, sweet thing," said an all-too-familiar male voice behind Irma. "Just you and me?"

"Martin!" Irma said, spinning around to

glare at the oh-so-geeky pest. "Disappear!"

Irma immediately turned back to her friends. Taranee had just rejoined them, carrying two cups of lurid pink punch. She handed one to Will.

"You know something, girls," Cornelia was saying. "I'd say that guy over there is cute enough for Elyon's punishment."

Elyon looked not at all unhappy at the prospect. In fact, she had that heavy-lidded, flushed-cheek look that screamed "boy crazy."

"I'm sure he gives great math lessons," Elyon cooed. She gave her friends a little good-bye wave and began making her way through the crowded gym to talk to the stranger.

"You go, girl," Irma cried with a laugh.

"Okay," Cornelia said, rubbing her fingertips together and turning to the group. "We're accepting bets on Elyon, ladies. I say she won't do it."

"Well, she did look pretty determined," Taranee said, taking a shy slurp of her punch. "What do you think, Will?"

"I . . . I . . ." Irma watched in alarm as Will's eyes went blank. She suddenly seemed overwhelmed by the crush of people around her.

Irma couldn't blame her. Some seventh-graders had started slam dancing nearby. A wacky kid in a Donald Duck costume was jostling Will as he pushed by with a platter of sandwiches on his head. And an enormous, surly-looking guy— must have been a football player—was looming over her in an ugly, blue, monster mask.

But then, Donald Duck slammed into the blue guy and knocked him back into the crowd, giving Will some space to breathe. It must have helped, because her eyelids fluttered and she seemed to shake the fog out of her head. Then she slowly grinned at her friends.

"I say Elyon can do it," she said. Irma felt a stab of affection for the scruffy new girl. First, she'd been the only one in the group who'd believed Irma's story. Now she was struggling to be cool, even though she was clearly freaked by the wildness of the party.

Cornelia must have sensed this, too, Irma grudgingly admitted to herself. Because she shot Will a look of concern.

"Everything okay?" she asked.

"I guess so," Will said, pressing a palm to one ear. "But don't you guys hear a strange humming noise, too?"

"The music is too loud," Taranee shouted. "Let's get away from here."

As the girls edged toward the door, Irma glanced over her shoulder, then blinked in surprise. Elyon—shy, sweet, awkward Elyon—was showing all the signs of expert flirtation. (And Irma certainly knew how to recognize them.) She was waggling her fingers at the new hottie and shooting him a lopsided grin. Irma even thought she saw Elyon wink.

But before Irma could get closer to spy on Elyon's close encounter of the cute kind, she heard a plopping noise. She spun around just in time to see Will lurch. She looked like she was about to faint!

"Uuuhhh," Will groaned. She'd dropped her cup of punch on the floor, and Taranee was grabbing her arm.

"Will," she exclaimed. "Do you feel okay?"

Will shook her head blearily. Over her head, Irma noticed that blue guy again. He was coming straight toward them.

Ewww! Irma thought. What a creep! Why doesn't he get lost? Then she returned her attention to Will, who looked a bit better.

"Just a short dizzy spell," Will was saying.

"Maybe a breath of fresh air would do me some good."

"We'll go with you," Cornelia said as Irma nodded.

Anything to get away from this scene and that pushy blue dude, she thought.

She was also still feeling a little cranky after the whole blue dress humiliation, not to mention two annoying buttinskies by the wretched Martin.

At least *he* seems to have evaporated, Irma thought. As she followed her friends out of the gym, she scanned the room. She didn't see a trace of the nerd-turned-mummy.

Well, Irma thought with a sigh, I guess this time, getting my wish was a good thing!

NINE

The Oracle was floating, suspended in a place both ethereal and solid—a platform that hovered in the very center of the Temple of Candracar. This was the Oracle's place of respite, where artwork created by a thousand otherworldly craftsmen decorated every inch of the walls; where the air was so thin and clean, it almost sparkled; where the Oracle's powers to see all, and know all, were at their most crystalline.

He knelt on the tiny platform, peace suffusing his face as he closed his eyes and focused his energy. His adviser, Tibor, stood sentinel behind him as always. Tibor's spine was ramrod straight and his eyes alert. His white beard and mustache were so long they nearly brushed against the Oracle's back. But the Oracle knew that age was irrelevant to Tibor's strength. The man was powerful. He was the brawn that allowed the Oracle to concentrate all his mental powers on the new Guardians, the young girls whom he had anointed to protect the Veil. Only this quickly thinning Veil separated evil—which had been exiled to the world of Metamoor—from good, which existed on earth.

If the girls failed at their mission, life as all knew it would be destroyed. The balance was growing more tenuous by the day—the Oracle could sense it. And the disruptive storms showering Heatherfield served as concrete warnings.

But the Oracle was not afraid.

For their salvation had begun.

In his unlined, outstretched hand, a small square suddenly appeared. It was a photograph of six girls. One wore an indigo dress, another, a flowing kimono. There was the mysterious one in an impish green costume. And then, of course, the one, the heart, she with the hair like flames and the sad, brown eyes.

"The new Guardians, Tibor," the Oracle

said. His voice sounded more like a dozen voices, all singing in harmony.

"Look at them!" the Oracle continued, gazing at the picture. "They are close."

"But not yet united," Tibor noted in his rumbly growl. The two gazed into the picture and saw the evil that lurked beyond its frame.

They saw Lord Cedric disguised in a stocking cap and a long cloak, which were both blue, the color of royalty. With him was the hulking monster Vathek. His skin was bright blue, his skull a lumpish monstrosity with beady, deep-set eyes. He loomed over the partygoers.

And then he spoke to his master. The Oracle could hear Vathek's words, though they were issued in the most guttural whisper.

"She's coming toward us, sir," Vathek said. He motioned with his scaly, blue chin toward the girl in green, the one called Elyon. The Oracle gazed at Elyon's shy smile. He read her thoughts: "He's so cute. He couldn't possibly be interested in someone as minor as me. But what do I have to lose?"

The Oracle almost chuckled at all that Elyon—and her friends—did not know.

"I'll take care of her, Vathek," Cedric whispered to his thug. His voice was as silky as a snake's hiss. "You think about the redhead. You know what to do."

"You can count on me, sir," Vathek said, baring his razorlike teeth in a grim smile. "In all this confusion, no one will notice me."

The music surged louder. The dancers grew more frenetic. The Oracle felt a stab of negative energy. At that moment, Lord Cedric and Elyon—the dark and the light—made their first contact.

"Umm, hi!" Elyon squeaked, waggling her fingers at the dark lord.

"Hello, Elyon," he replied. In the dim light, Elyon couldn't see the death in Cedric's icy blue eyes or the tightness of his smile. She did go wide-eyed, however, at the mention of her own name.

"You know my name?" Elyon said softly. "Who are you?"

"My name's Cedric," the evil lord replied.

Meanwhile, across the room, the outspoken one in the blue dress—Irma—was wielding power she didn't even know she had.

"Martin," she said to a hapless admirer behind her. "Disappear!"

And he did—literally going invisible in the blink of an eye. The Oracle could sense the boy's aura, continuing to move through the party, oblivious to his magical state of nothingness. There was no need to worry, the Oracle knew. This invisibility was only temporary.

Also oblivious was the heart, Will, who was swayed, but not conquered by the lurking presence of Vathek. He had come at her through the crowd, hurling toxic psychic waves in her direction.

The first time he'd lunged at her, he was intercepted by a boy with the head of a duck and a plate of food.

I almost had her! the Oracle heard Vathek think.

A few minutes later, Vathek made another pass, this time causing Will to drop her drink and waver, almost fainting. Her dizziness caused the Oracle to close his eyes and gird himself against a wave of pain.

As Will's friends whisked her out of the gym for fresh air, Vathek stormed after them in a rage. He pushed past a child who grinned at him and said, "Hey, cool costume, Bud!"

Humans! Vathek thought, his disdain searing the Oracle's mind. Maybe they wouldn't be so friendly if they knew that this is what I *really* look like.

Then something—or rather, *nothing*—stopped the blue brute in his tracks.

"Ouch!" cried a disembodied voice. Only the Oracle could see the spirit of the boy, the one wrapped in rags called Martin.

"Why don't you look where you're going, you big ox!" Martin yelled.

"Who . . . who said that?" Vathek growled, spinning around in confusion.

"I did!" Martin said. Suddenly, he shimmered into view, just as the Oracle had known he would.

"By the moons of Gaahn," Vathek said, invoking one of Metamoor's evil gods. "An invisible being!"

"Okay, so I'm not very popular here at school," Martin complained, glaring up at Vathek, "but you don't have to rub my nose in it."

Vathek gaped at Martin, who shrugged the disrespect away. He was used to it, the Oracle knew.

"In any case, great mask," Martin said, lifting his camera to his eyes. "You deserve a photo!"

His camera's flash exploded, bathing Vathek in a blast of light.

"Aaaaagh," the thug cried, clutching his enormous head. "My eyes! AAAARRRGGH! I can't stand light."

Vathek staggered heavily backward, crashing into a table of refreshments and sending drinks and bowls of potato chips flying. While nearby children screeched and leaped out of the way, Martin merely peered at his Polaroid as it developed in his hand.

"It came out a bit blurry, I'd say," Martin said.

Vathek growled. Smoke puffed out of his nostrils as he lunged for the skinny boy.

"You'll pay for this, microbe!" he growled. But, then, an echoing, amplified voice startled him out of his attack. It was the boy on the stage, the one Will had been gazing at admiringly.

"Your attention for a moment, guys," he yelled into his microphone. "Only three minutes left till midnight!"

An elderly woman in a voluminous robe and a large bubble of white hair took the microphone from the boy.

"And now it's time to burn the giant jack-o'-lantern in front of the school," the woman, the leader of these children, said. "But first, we'll award the prize for the best costume of the evening. And by unanimous vote, ladies and gentlemen, the winner is . . . that very large blue boy over there."

That would be the very large, blue Vathek, who was in the middle of contemplating his revenge against Martin.

"Let's see," Vathek was muttering. "I could turn you into a wart, but I'm not so sure that anyone would notice the difference—huh?"

With a start, Vathek noticed all eyes turning to him. And slowly, he comprehended the ridiculous fact that *he* had just won a Halloween costume contest. A crowd of chattering children grabbed the blue beast away from Martin and began shoving him through the gym door toward the giant pumpkin that rested on the front lawn.

"And there, on the grass," the Oracle said to Tibor, "the Guardians are waiting. The secret will soon be revealed, and the five will be together at last."

"Five?" Tibor said, peering over his master's

shoulder at the photograph in his hand. "I see six, sir."

"One of them will betray the others, my friend," the Oracle said quietly. "The moment they unite will also be the moment of betrayal."

TEN

Taranee gazed worriedly at Will, who was still a little shaky after her dizzy spell in the party. They were standing with Cornelia, Hay Lin, and Irma on the lawn just outside the gym door. And secretly, Taranee was relieved. The throbbing noise of the party and all those carefree, dancing people—they'd made her feel so out of place. The fact that most of these strangers wore costumes that blew away Taranee's simple, short-sleeved pink frock—*that* Taranee could handle. But dancing and totally letting go of all cares? Taranee had just never seen the point. She'd always been more comfortable being on the outside, peeking in. That was probably why she was happiest behind a camera, capturing the actions and images of other people.

Speaking of images, there was one out here that was totally creeping Taranee out—that giant papier-mâché jack-o'-lantern with its slit eyes and jagged grin. It was nothing but a big, fake pumpkin, but it made her shiver. Why did it seem so . . . sinister to her?

Taranee's brooding was interrupted by a chorus of whoops and yowls coming from inside the gym.

"And now what's going on?" she asked, watching anxiously as a crowd of people came tumbling out onto the lawn.

"It's the grand finale," Hay Lin explained. "The person with the best costume gets the honor of setting fire to the jack-o'-lantern."

Taranee watched as Mrs. Knickerbocker marched over to the jack-o'-lantern. She looked just like a circus tent in her billowing witch's robe and pointy black hat. High over her head she held an old-fashioned torch. Taranee was mesmerized by the violent, barely contained flame at the end of the torch. It looked so strong, almost as if it wanted to leap out of Mrs. Knickerbocker's grip. A plume of angry smoke billowed off the flame, clouding up the clear night air.

Close behind the principal, a bunch of kids were laughing and shoving that giant guy in the blue mask out of the gym.

Wow, that *is* some costume, Taranee thought. Those lumps all over his big, blue head are really disgusting. And he even got himself some big, blue hands with long, cracked claws. *Ewww.* They must be latex, but they sure look real.

For some reason, however, this kid wanted none of his "best costume" glory.

"Let me go!" he shouted, struggling to squirm away from the grip of half a dozen giggling kids. "Put me down. You're making a big mistake. You'll be sorry for this!"

"Halloween! Halloween!" the crowd was chanting. They formed a circle around the jack-o'-lantern, sweeping Taranee and her friends into their midst. The boy in blue staggered a bit. He gaped at the crowd as if he were an alien from outer space, encountering modern teen life for the first time.

What's up with this guy? Taranee wondered. She looked at her new friends. Hay Lin and Irma were jumping up and down and chanting along with the crowd: "Halloween! Halloween!"

Cornelia was smiling serenely, clapping in time to the chant. And Will was looking at the spectacle in a daze. Her shiny brown eyes reflected the red, dancing flames of Mrs. Knickerbocker's torch.

The principal turned to the reluctant honoree.

"Come on, be a sport," she said, reaching up and grabbing the guy's lumpy blue mask by one of its pointy ears. "Before we find out who's behind this great mask, how about getting our bonfire going?"

She held the torch out to the hulking, blue dude. But he only growled angrily in return.

"Oh, wow!" Taranee gasped. "He's giving the principal major lip! I wonder how much detention he's going to ge—*aaaaagh!*"

Taranee let out a little squeal as the blue boy did something even more shocking than talking back. He swatted the torch right out of Mrs. Knickerbocker's hand, sending it flying over his shoulder onto the papier-mâché pump-kin. Immediately, the jack-o'-lantern ignited.

"No one treats Vathek in this manner," he roared. "You have gone too far, you repulsive mass of cells."

Taranee sucked in her breath as Mrs. Knickerbocker stared at the hulking guy. She could see the principal's face move quickly from shock to cool dismissal.

"You're Samson, from homeroom 410, aren't you?" she said threateningly. "I recognize you, and I don't find you the least bit amusing."

Another big, thuggish boy stumbled out of a nearby cluster of partygoers. He was Frankenstein to a T—right down to the fake stitches in his forehead and the bolts poking out of his neck.

"Um, *I'm* Samson, ma'am," he said to Mrs. Knickerbocker.

"Huh?" the principal said in surprise. She turned slowly to the blue guy. And this time, Taranee thought she saw a flicker of fear in the old lady's eyes.

"So, who are you?" she demanded of the stranger.

Fwoooooom!

Before he could answer, a whoosh of hot air rushed out of the jack-o'-lantern. The small fire had really caught now. The flames began to crackle and leap several feet into the air.

But something was wrong.

This doesn't feel like some beachside bonfire, Taranee thought. She felt the hairs on the back of her neck stand up. She turned to her friends, wanting to describe the apprehension she felt. But she was speechless. She felt as if she were slogging through water, suppressed by slow motion. She could only stare at Will, her mouth open, her voice choked, her eyes wide with fear.

And she didn't have to wait long for that vague fear to be realized.

Ka-POW!

The scary-looking jack-o'-lantern exploded, sending rockets whistling into the black sky and shooting plumes of fire out toward the stunned crowd of kids.

The chaos was immediate.

"Aaaaaiggh!"

"Look out!"

"Everything's on fire!"

Like a panicked school of fish, the revelers began to fan out, getting as far away from the pumpkin as possible. Some ran back into the gym while others tore screaming into the street.

SSSssssss-FWOOOM!

The pumpkin unleashed another ominous set of explosions. Another firecracker zipped wildly through the air, trailing sparks. And the flames that engulfed the pumpkin grew hotter, higher, brighter.

But through the fire, Taranee could still see the outline of the jack-o'-lantern, and even its scary smile. Instinctively, she knew this was not the end. She began to think of the great pumpkin as a live being, an enemy, gearing up for a big finale.

Out of her peripheral vision, she saw Irma run and cower against the gym's outside wall. Cornelia gathered her billowing pink skirt around her and grabbed Hay Lin. The two scurried away from the pumpkin, stopping further out on the green lawn to turn and gape at the fiery spectacle.

Meanwhile, Will was staring at Taranee in horror.

"Let's get out of here, quick!" Will cried, starting to run after Cornelia and Hay Lin. That's when Taranee noticed the big blue thug.

He was right behind Will, running at top speed. But he didn't look as if he was fleeing like the rest of the kids. In fact, he was bearing down on Will. His eyes were squinty and malevolent.

"The girl!" Taranee heard him grunt. ". . . My chance!"

What's going on? a voice inside Taranee screamed. What does he want with Will? Why is this happening?

FWOOOOM-pop-pop-pop-pop!

With another tremendous roar, the jack-o'-lantern sent forth yet another flurry of rockets. Before Taranee could even react, one of them hit Will's attacker—right in his big blue butt!

"Yeow!" the guy screeched, his eyes going wild with pain. He reared back as Will ducked from beneath his grabbing hands. She had no idea that she'd even been in danger!

"Eeeeeek!"

Taranee spun around at the sound of the terrified shriek behind her.

Irma was clutching at the gym wall, screaming in terror as a rocket headed straight for her.

"Look out, Irma!" Taranee cried.

Once again, Taranee felt as if time had slowed down. She was aware of her hands flying into the air, reaching out for Irma. She could feel her eyes bulging in fear.

But this time, she wasn't speechless.

"STOP!" she cried.

Fzzzkzzzz.

Taranee gasped as the rocket—stopped! It hovered in midair, literally inches from Irma's nose. Irma stared, then squeezed her eyes shut and hunched her shoulders, preparing for the worst.

But Taranee wasn't going to let the worst happen. She felt something, like a band of energy, connect her with that sizzling rocket. She squinted at it. Every ounce of her being spoke silently to it.

And, somehow, for some reason, it obeyed her silent command. Taranee waved her arms upward. The firework followed the direction of her wave as if she were a puppeteer, and the rocket a marionette. It veered straight up, skimming past Irma and hurtling into the night sky.

Taranee gazed at the rocket, feeling a mixture of disbelief and incredible power. She had no idea what was happening inside of her. It was as if the front of her mind had checked out. She was all senses and intuition. And those were what had told her to speak to the rocket, to direct the fire.

But even thinking those things somehow caused the bond between Taranee and the rocket to break. She shook her head, as if coming out of a fog, and gazed at the rocket as it whirled and whistled through the sky. Taranee was dimly aware of Will standing a few feet away, bathed in the orange glow of the fiery pumpkin. She was just as transfixed by the soaring rocket.

And Will continued to stand there, paralyzed, as the rocket began to shoot back to earth. In fact, it was hurtling right back into the jack-o'-lantern from which it had first sprung.

BWWOOOOOMMM!

As the rocket made impact, the pumpkin's scary smile finally disappeared. In fact, the entire thing exploded in a huge, billowing burst of fire.

A rush of searing air accompanied the explosion. Taranee watched Will's face contort in horror as the heat knocked her peaked witch's hat from her head.

"Will!" Taranee screamed. Bursts of fire, resembling angry, orange claws, leaped out of the jack-o'-lantern. In another instant, those claws were going to engulf Taranee's friend. They were going to kill her!

Taranee threw her hands out in front of her, pushing against the angry heat with all her psychic might. She could hear her voice ring out. She was screaming. She was issuing an order.

"BACK!" Taranee cried.

And—the fire retreated.

Will collapsed onto the grass, her body bathed in the glow of flames that were perilously close, but no longer near enough to harm her. Gasping and sputtering, she crawled away from the fire just as Taranee's history teacher, Mr. Collins, dashed in and began to fight off the flames with a fire extinguisher.

Will gazed up at Taranee in shock. Hay Lin, Irma, and Cornelia stumbled over and stared at her, too.

"I think you owe us some kind of explanation, Taranee," Will said in a haggard whisper. "How . . . how did you do that?"

Taranee was staring at her hands. They had redirected a rocket. They had literally fought fire. But now they were only trembling.

"I don't know, Will," she squeaked. "I really don't know."

Will stumbled to her feet and threw her arms around Taranee. Her body shook with grateful sobs.

"You saved her life," Cornelia said, resting a gentle hand on Taranee's shoulder. Irma and Hay Lin also patted her comfortingly.

But Taranee merely stared over Will's shoulder at the dying flames of the jack-o'-lantern. What did I do? she thought, over and over.

And beneath that incessant question was another of even greater importance.

Who am I?

ELEVEN

Elyon leaned back against a tree in front of the school and sniffed the air. A full school day had gone by since the Halloween fire, but she could still smell acrid smoke in the air.

Even though she'd been inside the gym, flirting with Cedric when the fire had happened, she felt haunted by it. She could have died! Or the school where she'd been a student ever since kindergarten might have burned to the ground.

Most people would cheer at the idea. And sure, Elyon had made plenty of jokes with her friends about being cooped up in the Sheffield *Institution.*

But, she thought, fiddling idly with the tail of one of her straw-colored braids, I guess that fire made me realize something. Sheffield's sort of a second home to me.

She supposed if she felt a *little* closer to her parents, she wouldn't cling to her school so much. At least, that's what the Institute's counselor had told her once, during one of Sheffield's mandatory "check-ins."

Elyon rolled her pale blue eyes. Best not to go there. After all, there were so many more pleasant things to think about. Like Uriah and his gang stuck in detention for two weeks after it had been revealed that they'd planted fireworks in the jack-o'-lantern.

Elyon spotted the boys reporting to Mrs. Knickerbocker on the main lawn. They each held a huge garbage bag in which they'd collected singed leaves, papers, paper plates and cups, and whatever other gross garbage was left over from the Halloween party.

Ha, Elyon thought. Serves 'em right.

Her gaze lifted from the icky Uriah to the sky, which was clear, blue, and gorgeous.

Just like Cedric's eyes, Elyon thought with a sigh. She still couldn't believe that boy—an older boy with a beautiful face and long silky hair—had singled her out from all the girls at the party. He'd even asked around about her. He must have, or he wouldn't have known her name. And then he'd asked her that magic question. She still couldn't believe it. It was incre—

"Incredible!"

Huh? Elyon blinked in surprise as Irma uttered the very word that had just popped into her own head. She blinked a few more times and came back to earth, or rather, to this post-school gathering of girlfriends under Sheffield's biggest shade tree. Irma, Will, Hay Lin, and Taranee were lounging in a circle on the grass, while Cornelia was leaning against the tree with Elyon.

"It was all so real!" Irma was saying. "I don't know how to explain it. That place, those creatures, the sounds, the noises, even the smells. It was just like being there!"

"What's Irma talking about?" Elyon whispered to Cornelia. "I zoned."

"A dream she had last night," Cornelia whispered back. She had a slightly freaked look on her confused face—something between annoyed and bewildered. "She and Hay Lin were in some bizarre place—a sort of limbo between the Halloween party and the heavens. There was smoke everywhere. Plus a whole horde of demons who looked just like that creepy blue guy who started the fire."

"Hay Lin and I were just hanging on to each other," Irma was saying. "And then, suddenly, all these geometric shapes appeared in a mist over our heads. They were like enormous hieroglyphics. And in the middle was this sort of charm—a glass ball inside this curly bit of metal. And for some reason, that made me feel better. It was terrifying until that medallion charm-thing appeared."

Will leaned forward, her eyes wide.

"And then what happened?" she breathed.

"The alarm went off," Irma said, shrugging.

Elyon glanced at Hay Lin. She didn't seem to be paying any attention. In fact, she was doodling something on her palm with a Magic Marker. Elyon was surprised. Usually Hay Lin was, like, Ms. Supportive.

Finishing her sketch-on-skin with a flourish, Hay Lin thrust her hand beneath Irma's nose.

"Was the medallion anything like this?" she asked urgently.

Oh, Elyon thought. She peered over Irma's

shoulder to check out Hay Lin's inky palm. She'd drawn a pendant. Just as Irma had said, it had a clear orb in the center. Surrounding it was an incomplete circle. The top of it, around ten o'clock, swooped off into a little curlicue. And at the bottom, another little loop hung like a pendulum. At twelve o'clock, there was a ring—perfect for a chain.

Irma grabbed Hay Lin's hand and gasped.

"Gosh, yeah!" she said.

"Hang on a second," Will said, looking at Hay Lin's palm as well. "This is the same thing I dreamed about."

"You, too?" Irma breathed. She stared at Will, who nervously pushed a shock of red hair out of her eyes and blinked hard. Then she turned to Hay Lin, who was capping her marker and slipping it back into the pocket of her sweater.

"Neither Irma nor I have *ever* described it in such detail!" she said. "How did you know?"

"Simple," Hay Lin said with a smile. "I saw it in my dreams, too."

"Stop it! Just stop it!"

Elyon gasped and turned to look at Taranee. She'd been sitting by silently as Will, Irma, and

Hay Lin talked about the weird coincidence. But now, she was exploding.

"This . . . this is scaring me!" Taranee whimpered. "What's going on?"

That's when Cornelia sighed huffily and pushed herself away from the tree trunk. She planted her fists on her hips and scowled. Elyon clasped her hands and tuned in, feeling just a little grateful. All this talk was freaking *her* out, too. But finally, here was something familiar—Cornelia, taking charge.

"Let's reason here," Cornelia said. "Strange things have happened to just about all of us. Little things. Unexplainable ones that certainly aren't just our imagination!"

"And so, Sherlock?" Irma said impatiently.

"So, nothing!" Cornelia announced. She glanced around the Sheffield grounds. Besides Uriah and his detention crew, the grass was crawling with kids doing homework on laptops, Hacky Sacking—the usual after-school activities.

"Maybe we all need to talk it over calmly," she continued in a low voice. "But not here and not now!"

"Cornelia's right," Hay Lin said. She still had a little smile on her face.

Leave it to Hay Lin, who's still more interested in comic books than boys, Elyon thought,
to be psyched about supernatural phenome-
non. To her, it's just a game.

"How about meeting at my house this afternoon?" Hay Lin continued.

That made Elyon catch her breath.

"I don't know if I'll be there," she admitted.
Her voice trembled just a bit as she looked at
her friends' quizzical faces.

"Have you got something better to do,
Ellie?" Irma asked.

"Well . . ." Elyon said, feeling a smile spread
across her face. "I've got a date with Cedric!
That guy from last night, remember?"

"You don't say!" Cornelia said. Her scowl
had disappeared, and her blue eyes were
sparkling. "You convinced him to study with
you?!"

"He's so fascinating," Elyon said with a giggle. She knew she was blushing, but she didn't
care. "He invited me to his bookshop. He says
he has to talk to me!"

"A friendly little chat in a bookshop," Irma
said with a sneer. "Just thinking about it makes
me yawn."

"You're just jealous!" Elyon said, feeling cold resentment worm its way into her gut. Irma always had to be the center of attention!

"Is it that obvious?" Irma said with a mischievous smile.

"Oh . . ." Elyon said, feeling relief wash over her as quickly as her anger had. Irma had just been teasing.

"Ha!" Cornelia guffawed. "Don't worry about her, Elyon. We'd be the last ones to try to stop you!"

Elyon giggled and then, with exaggerated care, pulled up her sleeve to look at her watch. It was 3:45! She had to boogie.

Flashing her friends with a tremulous grin and a little wave, she trotted off the Sheffield grounds. She would have started skipping if she had been, like, eleven. But no, she was a teenager now, and she was on her way to a date.

Elyon rushed down Sixth Street toward Cedric's shop. She smoothed down her favorite green skirt and rustled her shaggy bangs just right. Then, she promptly tripped on a crack on the sidewalk.

"Oooh!" she grunted, catching herself with her hands before she took a major spill.

Oh, man, she thought as she scrambled to her feet. She carefully checked her bare knees. Scuffs—minimal, thank goodness. There was no way she could have shown up for the date with skinned knees. Cedric would think she was a total dweeb!

Elyon took a deep breath and approached the address Cedric had given her. She glanced up at the green sign hanging over the sidewalk—YE OLDE BOOKSHOP. This was it. Elyon checked her watch again.

"Four o' clock, sharp," she thought, taking quick shallow breaths. "I can do it! Take a deep breath and . . ."

Elyon reached for the big, brass doorknob and twisted it. The door opened with a creak. She poked her head into the store. Funny, how she'd never noticed this place before. It was amazing. The room was dark and shadowy and lined with flowery, Victorian wallpaper. There were Asian sculptures here and there, and, of course, tons of books, all of them ancient looking, bound in cracked leather, filling the air with that musty, dusty old book smell. Along the far wall was an amazing, round stained-glass window depicting a golden peacock.

"Umm, hello?" Elyon called squeakily. "Anybody here?"

"I'm right here, Elyon," a voice called from the back of the room. As Elyon crept into the store, letting the door fall shut behind her, Cedric stepped out of the shadows to stand in front of the glowing peacock window. He was holding an open book, looking quite the studious one.

Cedric had lost the stocking cap and the bad-boy mask. Now, his hair was pulled back into a low, loose ponytail, and his eyes were covered with hip, rectangular spectacles. He stood with perfect, even imperious, posture as he gazed over his book at Elyon.

Elyon felt her stomach lurch. If possible, Cedric looked even cuter than he had the night before. But she also noticed something else. His good looks had a glinty edge. His skin looked like fine porcelain, his eyes like cut sapphires.

He's too beautiful for me, Elyon thought.

Elyon shook her head quickly. Where had that come from? So what if Cedric was highly polished, making her feel all the scruffier? It also made her feel all the more flattered.

After all, out of all the girls at Sheffield—from elegant Cornelia to flirty, curvy Irma—Cedric had only asked *her* to the bookshop. He had singled out Elyon.

Only Elyon.

TWELVE

Hay Lin dropped a handful of green tea leaves into her mother's favorite red teapot, the one with the tiny partridge perched on the lid. Then she carefully poured boiling water from the kettle into the pot and watched the tea leaves billow and swirl in the stream. Beneath her kitchen's floorboards, she could hear the faint din of her parents' restaurant—the click of chopsticks on china, the sizzle of crisped rice hitting hot soup, the laughter of customers cracking open fortune cookies. It was a sound she'd grown up with, and it was as comforting to Hay Lin as chocolate milk or the perfect stuffed animal.

But this was no time to get nostalgic. Hay Lin needed to focus on the weird, magical dream that she and her friends had all had. Just the thought of the mysterious medallion made Hay Lin smile. Which was more than she could say for her pals. Cornelia, Irma, Taranee, and Will were all sitting around the big pine table in the cramped family kitchen, nibbling on her dad's crunchy almond cookies and looking seriously nervous.

It made sense that Hay Lin would be the cheerful one in the room. After all, she was the group's comic relief—she knew that. She was always ready with a big grin, a joke, an all-inclusive hug. It was easy for her. To Hay Lin every day was a little adventure, beginning with a fun foray into her closet. She'd find a bungee cord hanging from the doorknob and wrap it around her waist in a cool, crisscrossy pattern. She'd toss her long, blue-black hair under a pair of pink Elvis sunglasses, bunch some retro leg warmers around her ankles, and practically skip out the door.

When she was home, she had anchors all around her—her drawing pencils and paints, her comic books, the whispered conversations she had with her grandmother about, oh, everything. Grandma liked to fill Hay Lin's head with all sorts of stories. She told her that every flower was a vessel for a human soul; that crickets meant the best of luck; that a messy room indicated a creative mind; that magic lurked around the edges of everyday life.

Hay Lin didn't actually believe that. Grandma's magic was like a Buddhist Santa Claus—something fun for Hay Lin to dream about, even cling to, on the rare occasions when she felt adrift.

And Hay Lin did have to admit, she'd been feeling just a *little* floaty lately. After all, she was the only one of her friends who'd never had a crush. She thought talking about boys was fun and all, but it didn't make her get all gushy and moist-eyed and faraway. She would look around her classes at Sheffield and stare at this boy or that. All she saw were their knobby knees and sunken chests and chewed-on fingernails; the way they spewed Fritos in the lunchroom and laughed like donkeys. She found boys totally resistible.

They were also a source of the tiniest gap between Hay Lin and her buds.

Not that it was a biggie. Hay Lin knew her hormones were gearing up. And to tell the truth, she could stand the wait. In her book, things were pretty much fine as they were.

Especially now, when Cornelia, Irma, and the new girls were all glancing at one another anxiously and whispering about unexplainable things.

Welcome to my world, girls, Hay Lin thought as she filled five red cups with steaming, fragrant tea.

"So, what do you think the explanation is?" Taranee was saying.

Hay Lin shrugged and looked at her friends' bewildered faces.

"Well, it's not like there has to be an explanation," she said lightly.

"No!" Cornelia said, anxiously turning a cookie around and around in her long, slender fingers. "There's a reason behind everything, and I want to know what's going on! And by the way, I want you all to know that I don't believe in magic or paranormal phenomena."

Hay Lin turned to put the teapot on the counter and rolled her eyes. That's Cornelia, she thought. Always in control. Well, until now, maybe.

"Mysterious dreams, clothes that change

color, flying objects, premonitions," Taranee listed, her voice getting quieter with each item. "What do you call these?"

"Growing pains?" Irma interjected, grinning through a mouthful of cookie.

"Maybe that medallion is the answer we're looking for," Will said with a shrug.

Hay Lin glanced at the smudgy drawing on her palm and remembered something. She grabbed her book bag from the corner where she'd tossed it and pulled a sheet of paper out of it. Then she hurried back to the table to show it to Will and Irma.

"Look, I've sketched a better copy of the medallion," she said. "I hope I didn't forget anything."

Hay Lin felt a little thrum of pride as Will raised her eyebrows at her drawing. She knew she was a good artist—always had been. The charm's silvery setting, its craggy glass orb— they looked positively 3-D.

"I'd say it's all there," Irma said, nodding as she grabbed another cookie.

"Hmmm," Will said. "Yep, that looks a lot like it."

Suddenly, Hay Lin heard a faint swishing

at the doorway. It was the trademark rustle of the traditional Chinese robe her grandmother always wore. And when Hay Lin looked up, of course, there her grandmother was. Her copious wrinkles were scrunched into a sly smile.

Hay Lin's own welcoming smile faded a bit as she saw her grandmother pull something out of her pocket. It was a necklace. With a charm. A charm that looked shockingly familiar.

"Grandma!" she cried.

"That's it!" Will said. "The medallion from our dreams. Where did you get it?"

"What matters," Hay Lin's grandmother said to Will in her scratchy, high-pitched voice, "is that you will be keeping it now. This is the Heart of Candracar."

Grandma's sharp, heavily wrinkled eyes swept over the five girls.

"And you are the new Guardians," she announced, gripping the medallion's chain tightly. Hay Lin felt her skin prickle. She'd never seen this side of her grandmother. She'd always been powerful, but quiet, acting from the sidelines. Now, she stood over their group with palpable power, like a queen.

For the first time since all this magic had begun, Hay Lin felt fear.

"Wh-what are you talking about?" she quavered.

Grandma smiled at her reassuringly and motioned for Hay Lin to sit down with the others. Then she stood at the head of the table and began to speak.

"Let me tell you a story, girls," she said. "A story as old as time—a distant time when everything was young, and spirits and creatures lived under the same sky."

Hay Lin felt the familiar tug of comfort that her grandmother's tall tales always gave her. But fighting that contentment was the creeping knowledge that this time, the story might be . . . real?

"The universe was a single, immense kingdom ruled by nature," Grandma continued. "A kingdom that lasted eons. Until . . ."

Grandma paused dramatically before she said, "Spirits and creatures learned evil, and this one world was divided into those who wanted peace and those who lived on others' pain. To separate the two halves, the Veil was created. Evil and injustice were banished to the dark side of Metamoor, which had once been one of the universe's most beautiful worlds."

Hay Lin knew her mouth was hanging open and her hands were trembling. But she didn't care. She could only try to wrap her brain around this incredible news that her grandmother was delivering.

"Before separating for eternity," Grandma explained, "the universe gave life to the Temple of Candracar, in the very heart of infinity. There, the mightiest spirits and creatures are on guard. There, the protectors of the Veil reside and there, if you wish, you also may journey."

Hay Lin gasped and shook her head. Her grandma hadn't just said that they could take a field trip to the heart of infinity—had she? And what *was* the "heart of infinity"?

"It is not by mere chance that you are here," Grandma intoned, pausing to look each girl in the eye, one by one. "You are the new Guardians of the Veil. The most important warriors in a battle that began thousands of years ago."

"The Veil?" Irma piped up.

"The world is made of many different worlds, and the Veil is what divides them," Grandma explained. She held the medallion—the Heart of Something-a-car, Hay Lin told herself—and gave it a reverent look. Then she turned back to the girls, her eyes suddenly flashing darkly.

"It is a barrier that has become dangerously fragile," she said hoarsely. "There are portals between the world of evil and the world that is ours. And those portals are being breached."

Hay Lin saw Will's lip tremble as she spoke up.

"I—I'm afraid I don't understand," she said.

Grandma nodded kindly.

"To understand," she said, "listen to your two hearts. One beats within you, and the other is the Heart of Candracar."

As Grandma spoke, the medallion that she held above her head began to shimmer. Then it trembled. And suddenly, it let loose a burst of light that quickly settled into a warm, pulsating glow. Grandma stepped over to Irma, who gasped as she fixed her eyes on the glowing medallion.

"The forces of nature lie within, and from now and forever, they will be with you," Grandma said to the group. Then she looked down at Irma, smiling kindly.

"You, Irma," she said, "will have power over water—broken and uncontainable."

Hay Lin saw Irma's eyes light up—or maybe that was just the reflection of the glowing, glass orb. In any case, her expression quickly went dark again as Hay Lin's grandmother stepped over to Cornelia, who looked as if she were fighting the urge to leap up from the table and run far, far away.

"To you, firm Cornelia, the power of earth," Grandma pronounced, before turning to Taranee. "And to you, generous Taranee—the difficult gift of fire."

Finally, Grandma stepped over to Hay Lin and placed her dry, warm hand on top of her head. Hay Lin felt herself relax and smile at her grandma's touch. Even in this, the most confusing moment ever, Grandma was a steadying presence.

"And you, my little Hay Lin," Grandma crooned softly. "You will be free and light as air."

Hay Lin's eyes flapped open. She was sure she'd felt a cool breeze skim over her face the minute the word "air" had left Grandma's mouth. She blinked in amazement, before her attention shifted to Will.

"And me?" Will said tremulously, gazing up at Grandma.

"Give me your hand, Will," Hay Lin's grandmother said. Obediently, Will held out her palm. As Grandma slowly lowered the Heart of Candracar into it, she said, "You will find out soon enough."

The medallion came to a rest on Will's palm. Then its warm, pulsing glow began to grow. It became more and more intense until the orb was shooting beams of sparkling, silver light all over the kitchen. Hay Lin held her breath and tried not to scream.

But Will didn't seem scared at all. In fact, she seemed transformed. She still looked the same, skinny Will, swimming in a pair of blue corduroy overalls, but her face was rapturous. Her hair was floating around her head in a luminous halo. And her hand, clasping the magical Heart of Candracar, seemed to float upward.

"Aaagh!" Will cried, throwing her head back. Hay Lin didn't know *what* was surging through her new friend. Pleasure? Power? Knowledge? Or . . .

"This, this is magic!" Irma breathed.

Hay Lin glanced at Irma and nodded. That's exactly what it was.

And it was also, suddenly, over. Hay Lin's broken gaze, or Irma's voice, or *something* seemed to have broken the spell. The Heart of Candracar became, once again, an inert charm. And Will had returned to being ordinary Will, albeit a very shaken up one.

She turned to gaze at Hay Lin's grandmother, but Grandma was already halfway out the door. Hay Lin bit her lip. She knew this routine. When Grandma was done talking, she was *done talking*. There was no cajoling her to stick around.

So she knew it was a lost cause when Will called to her grandmother's retreating mane of silver hair, "Just a moment. Wait! Don't go away!"

But Grandma had already slipped into the hallway, which was the central artery of Hay Lin's apartment. From that hallway, everything led—bedrooms and bathrooms, her parents' business office and the stairs down to the restaurant. Each door was shut, and Grandma was nowhere to be seen. She'd as good as disappeared.

Hay Lin gently put an arm around Will's shoulders and led her toward the stairs. The rest of the girls followed in silence. No one said a word until they'd formed a small, tight circle on the sidewalk outside the restaurant's big round front window.

"I don't completely understand what just happened," Taranee said wanly.

"Nothing happened!" Cornelia retorted as she arranged her hot-pink shrug around her shoulders. Then she glared at Hay Lin.

"With all due respect, Hay Lin, I think your grandma has a few screws loose," she said. "She told us that ridiculous story, hoping that she'd amaze us using that trick with the shining medallion."

"You're *afraid*, Cornelia, aren't you?" Irma said, giving her a smirk.

Cornelia rolled her eyes and spun on her heel, walking toward the corner. She tossed some parting words over her shoulder, not to mention a glare reserved just for Irma. Irma always got under Cornelia's skin. They were so different! Like fire and ice.

Make that earth and water, Hay Lin thought with a gulp.

Cornelia turned. "I don't believe in fairy tales, Irma," Cornelia called. "This is different. And now, I'm going home."

Taranee glanced at Hay Lin in alarm. Hay Lin, too, felt worried for an instant. Then she shook it off. This was Cornelia. She was just mad that she hadn't figured this all out herself. But she was never one to abandon her friends.

"I know her," Hay Lin said to the remaining girls. "She'll change her mind."

After Cornelia had rounded the corner, Irma turned back to the group, looking a little stunned. But quickly, her trademark grin returned.

"Hey, if we're some kind of supergroup, we should have costumes, don't you think?" she said. Then she giggled and balled up her fists to make her biceps bulge. Not that they bulged that much.

Hay Lin laughed and did a little karate chop in Irma's direction. Then she looked around their little group and gasped. She'd just realized something.

She pulled her felt-tip pen out of her cardigan pocket and began writing on her palm. Then she gazed at the word she'd written there, amazed at how everything seemed to be falling into place.

"We need a name, too," Hay Lin said. "And check this out—what do you think about W.i.t.c.h.? It's our initials put together? Will, Irma, Taranee, Cornelia, Hay Lin! Isn't that cute?"

Taranee gazed at her and clasped her hands behind her back.

"All that ink is going to end up poisoning you, Hay Lin," she said drily.

"It's already poisoned her," Irma cried, grabbing Hay Lin's hand and looking scornfully at the smudgy acronym. "W.i.t.c.h.! I've never heard of anything so dumb. I don't feel like a witch."

Irma turned to Will. They all looked at Will.

"I— I don't know. I'm still a bit confused," Will managed to say, shakily. Hay Lin saw what could only be described as awe in her big, brown eyes.

And that's when Hay Lin remembered exactly what her grandmother had said. They were all Guardians, all elements—earth, air, water, fire. Except Will. She was special. She was the keeper of the Heart of Candracar. Hay

Lin didn't know what that meant, but she suspected it made Will their leader, in some way.

What sort of battle Will would lead them in, though, Hay Lin couldn't begin to imagine.

THIRTEEN

Hours had gone by since the events of the Halloween party, but still the Oracle sat. He was cross-legged and contemplative in the Temple's most sacred space, the mile-high shaft that formed the core of the Temple of Candracar.

Standing behind him—as always—was Tibor. But, for the first time in perhaps a century and a half, the old man's white beard was parted by a smile. He was gleeful.

"Oracle," he exclaimed, "now they are together."

And indeed they were. The Oracle had transposed his vision of the five newly anointed Guardians into the air before them. The girls' awestruck faces floated

within a halo of green flame. It was there that Tibor could watch the visions that the Oracle saw in his mind.

"And so, our waiting is over," the Oracle said, nodding peacefully.

Without using his hands or Tibor's help, the Oracle rose gracefully to his feet. The Guardians' image evaporated into a wisp of vapor that unleashed a flurry of scents—ocean water, a floral breeze, a hint of smoke, rain-damp earth.

Then, the Oracle turned to greet his guest— a tiny woman in flowing Chinese robes standing at the sanctuary's door. Her hair was long and white; her ears, large and ever vigilant; her face, at rest in a contented, creased smile.

"The congregation is grateful to you, Honorable Yan Lin," the Oracle said to the air Guardian's grandmother. The old woman smiled wider and bowed her head to her lord.

"Your task is complete," the Oracle continued. He glanced back at Tibor. His ancient adviser fairly glowed with hope. "The waiting is over. We can begin."

FOURTEEN

Will gazed at the questioning eyes of Irma, Hay Lin, and Taranee. She glanced to her right and saw her reflection in the round window of the Silver Dragon—she looked pale and trembly and a bit small, which was exactly how she felt. At least, she wasn't seeing that alternate self, the one with the long legs and the knowing eyes and the wings. *That* would have been way more than Will could handle right now.

In fact, she couldn't even handle Irma's simple question: how did she feel about giving their group the name W.i.t.c.h.?

She looked at her new friends and suddenly felt as if they were very far away. She could barely comprehend all the things Hay

Lin's grandmother had just unloaded on them. But one thing was clear. They were all—what was it called? Guardians. But while four of them had these superpowers of air, water, fire, and earth, Will had absorbed the Heart of Candracar. What kind of power did she have now? She didn't know what the pendant meant. All she knew was it made her different from the other girls.

She was alone.

As usual.

"Guys!"

Will's brooding was interrupted by an elated voice. The girls all turned to see Elyon bounding down the sidewalk across the street.

"Look who's here," Taranee said.

"Elyon!" Irma called as their giddy bud dashed across the crosswalk and hopped over to them. "Is your date already over?"

"Only round one," Elyon said, breathing hard and grinning. "Cedric wants to see me tonight in the school gym."

"I can think of more romantic places," Hay Lin said, rolling her eyes at Irma.

"He said it was just the right place to tell me

a special secret," Elyon gushed, her cheeks flushing.

"Oh, if that's the case," Irma said, winking back at Hay Lin, "there are less ridiculous excuses."

Suddenly, Elyon went pale, and her blue eyes clouded over a bit. Will bet she knew exactly what she was feeling. The initial elation of her triumph had worn off, and now Elyon was good and scared. Will had *so* been there before.

"Why don't you go with me?" Elyon suddenly said. "With you guys there, I'd feel more comfortable."

When you're right, you're right, Will thought, smiling to herself.

Irma nodded enthusiastically.

"Never deny a friend a favor," she announced, "especially if she lets you stick your nose in her business!"

"Same goes for me," Hay Lin said.

"I'll be there, too, Elyon," Will said to her own surprise. Then she shrugged.

Why not? she thought. It's better than sitting home, brooding about suddenly being a magical freak!

"And you, Taranee?" Elyon asked, turning

to smile at the last member of the group. "You'll come, too, won't you?"

"I don't think so," Taranee said wistfully. "My folks will never let me go out tonight. I just went out last night!"

Irma slung one arm around Will's shoulders and the other around Hay Lin's. Giving them each a squeeze, she announced to Elyon, "That makes three of us. Do you think that'll do?"

"Yeah, I think that'll do," Elyon said with an emphatic nod. "That'll do just fine."

Will sighed and looked at her new friends, giggling, teasing one another, bonding in a big way. And she realized—she was a part of it! They weren't excluding her just because she was the keeper of the Heart of Candracar.

Whatever scary stuff comes our way now, we'll help one another through it, Will thought. We're *all* Guardians. And maybe I'm not as alone as I thought.

It's a good thing I'm not alone, Will was thinking a few hours later. This is creepy!

She, Irma, and Hay Lin had just arrived at Sheffield's front gate. It was gently swinging back and forth on its hinges, making a faint, eerie, squeaking noise. The whole school was dark. Only a bright, full moon provided a hazy, blue glow on the grounds.

"The gate is open," Hay Lin pointed out. She snuggled deeper into her puffy, blue down coat. It had gotten chilly tonight.

"Elyon must already be here," Will said. "Let's go in, too."

The three girls scurried down the walkway to the gym doors. Will pushed them open and took a few, faltering steps into the gym. Not one light was on. Hay Lin and Irma hovered inside the doorway.

"Elyon?" Will called. Her voice sounded faint as it echoed through the big, and seemingly empty, space. "Are you here?"

"Elyon is at home, sleeping," Irma said, shivering. "Trust me. It's pitch-dark in here. Let's go!"

"Irma is right," Hay Lin whispered. "M-m-maybe it's all a big joke."

Will turned around and stumbled to the wall next to the door. She felt around, looking for a switch plate or fuse box. But nothing beneath her fingertips felt familiar, except that cold, clammy feeling of painted cinder block.

"If only I could manage to turn the lights on," she muttered.

"Aaaaiiigh!"

Will gasped as she heard her friends scream in terror. She spun around just in time to see the gym doors slam shut. Even the faint glow from the moon disappeared, and, for a horrible instant, Will felt as if she were floating in space. She had no sight, no senses, nothing to anchor her.

But quickly, almost . . . magically, Will's eyes adjusted to the light. She almost wished they hadn't, because, through the hazy gloom, she saw Hay Lin and Irma squirming in the clutches of a monster!

Will gasped as she looked at the creature. It was *the* monster—the one that had acted so weird at the Halloween party the night before. A wave of fear washed over Will. That had been no kid in an ugly blue costume.

This monster was for real.

And he'd changed for the worse.

For one, he'd gotten bigger. He must have been more than seven feet tall now, and he had the girth of a refrigerator. The lumpy, rock-like bumps on his head had become full-fledged horns—sharp and threatening. His tiny teeth had turned into huge, yellow, lethal fangs.

He was effortlessly holding Hay Lin and Irma with one beefy arm. Irma kicked wildly at him with her red Hush Puppies, but she barely even connected.

"Let me go, you big ape," Irma shrieked. "If this is a joke, it's not funny."

But the monster didn't let go. In fact, it looked like he was squeezing them tighter.

"Welcome, Guardians."

Will gasped. A disembodied voice—gravelly and hissing, positively snaky—wafted over to them. Will glanced away from her struggling friends for an instant to scan the shadowy gym. Where was that voice coming from? She couldn't see anybody. But clearly, that somebody could see them. And . . . he knew who they were. He'd called them Guardians.

This *cannot* be good, Will thought in panic.

"Wh-what do you want?" she called out into the darkness. She saw Hay Lin and Irma stop kicking and grunting for a moment. This was big. This was information they needed to know.

As the horrible, reptilian voice bellowed his answer, Will felt her heart sink.

"I want to destroy you, Guardians," the voice said simply. "To destroy you and take over your world!"

Will felt as if she were drowning. She clawed at her chest, struggling for air. Finally, her lungs rescued her, making an involuntary gasp for oxygen. Will took a deep, shuddery breath, clasping her hands over her gut.

And that's when she felt something hard and warm beneath her right hand. It pulsated. In fact, it almost hurt. The thing's heat—its energy—was intense.

"By now, the Veil is weak, and without you, victory will be easy," the voice roared. "When a millennium comes to an end, the Veil's weaving loosens. Light filters through its pores, piercing through our darkness. And it is then that we see the portals that lead to your world."

"Weak?" Will whispered. The heat in her palm was searing now. It pricked at her, sending jets of energy up her arm. In fact, she felt as if the heat had entered her bloodstream. It was a feeling her body couldn't recognize. It was both awful and glorious.

Through the haze of this experience, Will heard the blue creature growl, "What shall I do with them, Master?"

"Tear open a pit and throw them in, Vathek," the voice responded.

"Help!" Hay Lin shrieked. She and Irma began screaming and squirming, trying fruitlessly to wrench themselves free from this horrible creature.

Will's mind seemed to shut down. She could hear herself breathing and feel her heart thumping slowly inside her chest. But most of all, she could feel energy shooting from her curled fist to all points of her body. Slowly, she willed her fingers to open.

And when they did, the medallion—glowing brilliantly—was resting on her palm.

"That's what it was," a voice inside Will's head said triumphantly. "The Heart of Candracar. Maybe this is the time to use it."

Her hand seemed to take over. And it knew just what to do.

"Hay Lin, Irma!" Will called, throwing the Heart of Candracar to her friends with a sweeping motion. "Water! Air!"

As the medallion soared through the air,

Will saw the glass orb that was its center seem to separate into three, vibrating, tear-shaped missiles. One became liquid and swirly. It landed in front of Irma. It hovered before her stunned eyes and then began to weave its way around her body, as if it were wrapping her in invisible ribbon.

The medallion also seemed to wrench Irma from the blue creature's grip. As she sprang away from him, he howled in rage.

The exact same thing happened to Hay Lin, except the teardrop that danced around her was almost like a vapor, a puff of shimmering air.

And finally, there was Will's teardrop. It throbbed before her eyes and turned a shocking pink. It pulsed like a beating heart.

Will felt her fear melt away. She reached out to the heart, beckoning it to come to her. And then it, too, began to swirl around her body.

Out of the corner of her eye, Will saw Hay Lin gasp with joy and throw her arms over her head. She looked as if she were feeling true freedom for the first time. Her hair came free of her goggles and began to twist around her torso like a glossy, black cyclone.

Irma's hair floated up from her scalp, and

her eyes turned sultry and mischievous. Before Will's very eyes, Irma's lips went pouty, her clothes melted away, and feathers unfurled from her back.

And that's when Will ceased to see her friends. Because she was going through her own incredible transformation. Her back arched, and her body shook, as if she were having a seizure. Will felt a wave of heat shoot through her. The energy she'd felt in her veins became stronger now. It filled her body until it seemed like her real self must have disappeared, leaving behind only a soul, floating in space.

But that wasn't possible, because Will suddenly felt her body hunch forward. She hugged her knees, curling into a ball.

This is just like the dream I had in the car, Will realized.

Then she felt a tugging on her back. Instinctively, she knew she was growing wings, just as Irma had. She was becoming the beautiful woman she'd seen in the bookshop window and in her bedroom mirror. She felt her limbs lengthening, her face changing, her muscles growing lean and strong.

Will felt a calm suffuse her as she burst out of her coiled position and leaped into a fighting stance.

With that one pouncing motion, Will accepted her fate. She was no longer just a student, just a daughter, or just a friend. She was a Guardian of the Veil, the keeper of the Heart of Candracar.

And life as she'd known it—for better or worse—had changed forever.

IRMA IS RIGHT! M-M-MAYBE IT'S ALL A BIG JOKE!

ELYON! ARE YOU HERE?

ELYON IS AT HOME, SLEEPING. TRUST ME! IT'S PITCH-DARK IN HERE! LET'S GO!

IF ONLY I COULD MANAGE TO TURN THE LIGHTS ON!

AAAAHH

WELCOME, GUARDIANS!

LET ME GO, YOU BIG APE! IF THIS IS A JOKE, IT'S NOT FUNNY!

AAAGH!

TO BE CONTINUED . . .